A Stark and Stormy Night

Paul G. Brand
~ and ~
Craig A. Hart

Sweatshoppe Publications

A Stark and Stormy Night

© 2016 Paul G. Brand and Craig A. Hart

ISBN 10: 1534905162

ISBN 13: 978-1534905160

The night filled the alley between Harry's Bar and the Motel de la Mer. It was a dark night, rainy and full of rats, the kind of night that went out looking for trouble and dragged it into alleys by the hair of its ballsack. The rain spattered on the ground and rolled in thin streams off the corners of buildings like tears down the cheeks of jilted lovers. Thunder trembled in looming cloudbanks that lit up sporadically as flickers of lightning stabbed through them.

I once lived in the Mer. The place so crawled with fleas that I spent more time next door in Harry's getting loaded than in my room getting laid. And more time scratching my itching ass than getting loaded. Motel de la fucking Mer. It took people with no class to think they could slap a fancy name on something and make it classy. Every night, the soundtrack repeated itself: a dozen scraps and just as many night cats fucking their stooges. Sometimes it was the same show at the same time and with the same actors. Lots of broads ankled down the dank hallway, their mugs all beat to hell, their veiny claws clutching cabbage. It got me riled, but the pro skirts knew their business. Still, it wasn't kosher to hit a dame.

Yeah. Classy joint. I moved out as soon as I had two dimes to scrape together.

I had one friend at the Mer, a bona fide wordsmith. He spent all day and night tapping away on his beat-up old typewriter, trying to break into the movie racket. I didn't know his real name. Nobody did. So I called him Tolstoy. We played poker on Thursday nights. I let him win most of the time to keep his spirits up and help him make the rent. My wallet was thin, but his was thinner. It was Thursday. And that was why I'd been walking through the alley between Harry's Bar and the Mer on a dark, rainy, rat-filled night. And I would've kept walking, right up to Tolstoy's room, if I hadn't stumbled over a dead body. It was a woman and she'd been shot. The night was full of rats, alright, and one of them had a gun.

She lay on her back, staring up like she was about to ask me a question. I had a few questions too, but she wasn't talking. Not to me, not to nobody. She'd been killed by a single bullet and lay naked as an unwrapped lollipop and looking just as sweet. Except for that ugly hole. The one just above her left tit. Her tits sat on her chest like lumps of uncooked bread dough with a ripe strawberry pointing out of each one. She had curves, this one, dangerous curves. It was such a waste that I got pissed off. Her eyes, green like those fancy jewels—the green ones—were wide and begged me for help. Red lipstick, the reddest, covered her mouth.

I felt something on my shoe and looked down. A rat, a big ugly fucking rat with a big ugly fucking tail. It made a move for the woman's mug and I swear to Christ I heard it click its big ugly fucking teeth. I kicked at it, missed, got pissed off again, and pulled out my heater. I pumped lead and splattered that son of a bitch all over the wet concrete. I hated rats. I couldn't help the dame, but I didn't have to let a fucking rat eat out her eyeballs. I took off my overcoat and put it over her body. I'd be lying if I said I didn't take a final look at those tits.

Having made her decent, I beat it for the Mer and walked into Tolstoy's room without knocking.

"A little late, aren't you?" he said.

I could tell he was sore. He sat at a card table playing Solitaire and, if I knew Tolstoy, cheating. He wore his customary hat, a ratty old green felt derby, ugly as your father's balls, all dented up and smelling of cigarettes and anxious sweat. It sat low over his brows, shadowing his beady little eyes. When I saw him sitting there, I wondered, as I did every time, why I kept coming here. Tolstoy looked a little like a rat himself. But he was *my* rat and I felt responsible.

"I need to use the horn," I said.

"I don't have a phone. You know that."

"There's gotta be one around here somewhere."

"There's a house phone in the hall, but Miss Foxy charges a nickel after five."

"Fuck that." I ran down the hall and grabbed the phone. "Operator, gimme the cops."

Tolstoy watched me from his doorway. "The cops?"

"The cops?" the operator said.

"Yeah, the cops," I said.

"Why are you calling the cops?" Tolstoy shouted. "Does this have something to do with the gunshots I heard a minute ago?"

"What's that?" said the phone. I recognized the voice. It was O'Riley, the desk sergeant. "You heard gunshots?"

"Are you on a case?" Tolstoy took great interest in my cases, even trying to convince me to take him on as a partner. "I could be your Dr. Watson," he'd say. "I'd write down your adventures. We'd be an excellent team!"

"It ain't about the shot," I said.

"Then why ya callin' us, buddy?" O'Riley said. "We're busy down here! A dark and stormy night like this brings all the rats out!"

"You're telling me," I said. "I just sent one rat to hell. And another just shot a dame."

"A dame's been shot?" Tolstoy said. He scurried down the hall and plucked at my sleeve. I shooed him away. "So you *are* on a case!"

"Say, who is this?" O'Riley said. "Raving, that you? What'd you do this time?"

"This isn't about me; it's about a body in an alley."

"It's always about you, Raving. You always find a way to make it about you. That's why you never made it as a cop."

"Ancient history, O'Riley. That's water under the bridge."

"I'm glad to hear you say that. I'd thought you still harbored some resentment, but it's good that you see it as a thing of the past."

"It'd be a lot easier if the department would stop holding it over my head."

"Well, it's all still a matter of record. And what really happened is common knowledge."

"Yeah, but there's no use cryin' over spilled milk," I said. "What's done is done. We need to move past it and look to the future."

"Indeed. As long as we learn from history so—"

"—we ain't doomed to repeat it. I know, I know," I said. "Just get over here and collect the stiff. Do your job before the rats do theirs."

"Where's the body?"

"In the alley between Harry's Bar and the Hotel de la Mer."

"I know the place. I'll send a car. Don't go anywhere, Raving. We'll have a few questions for you."

"I can't wait." I slammed the phone back onto the cradle.

"There's a body outside?" Tolstoy said. "Sweet mother of Christ! A real live body! This is just what I need for my screenplay!" He bounded toward the front door.

"It's a real live *dead* body," I said. "Don't touch a fuckin' thing!"

When I caught up to Tolstoy, he was standing over

the body, staring and kneading his ugly hat. The thing already looked like his old man's loving paternal ballsack and he wasn't doing it any favors the way he was manhandling it.

"What's the matter, pal, ain't you never seen a corpse before?" I dropped a hand on his shoulder, and he nearly jumped out of his overcoat.

"Jesus!" he squeaked. He screwed the hat back onto his head.

"Not round here, he ain't. Jesus was a smarter than that. Wanna head up to Ariel's? Cab fare's on me."

"I...um. N-no, no thanks. I'm just going to..." Tolstoy trailed off, still staring at the dead dame. The staring part made sense, but he was being too goddamn twitchy for my liking.

"What the hell, Tolstoy? A minute ago, you couldn't wait to see a stiff. Make up your mind, willya?"

Little bastard didn't even blink.

"Maybe you better sit this one out. Go back on upstairs and smith some words, huh?" I steered him back toward the Mer's rusty wrought iron bannisters and aimed him at the front door. Guy moved like he was under water, but at least he was headed in the right direction. Good enough for me.

Back in the alley, I saw a couple rats, their wet black fur glistening under the street lamp, calmly eating the remains of their recently exploded comrade.

"Fuckin' monsters," I grumbled. I could hear the sirens now. I squinted through the sheets of rain and saw the clumsy dance of the cruisers' red lights painting the sodden streets crimson with a drunkard's brush.

Good.

Normally, I'd be pissed, having a swarm of cops crawling all over one of my jobs, but this wasn't gonna be one of my jobs. I'd seen a lot in my life, but when some hood drills a dame right in the tit like that, it—well, let's just say I'd rather not have this one on my plate.

The cars pulled into the alley, their headlamps lighting up the place like the Second Coming of our fucking Lord. I squinted and shaded my eyes with my right hand.

"Raving, is that you?" one of the cops called out. "If it ain't, get your fuckin' hands up!" Through the glare of the lights, I could see he had his gun pointed at me.

"Yeah, it's me," I said, raising my hands just to be safe. I knew this cop. McCarthy. He was a real crusader. It wouldn't do to mess with an itchy trigger finger. Not on a night like tonight. Not with all these rats around.

"Well, shit, ya beat us to this one, Raving. This your case?"

"Not mine," I said. "I kinda stumbled over her."

McCarthy approached, followed by his buddies. He looked around.

"Huh, I thought Cassidy'd be here by now. This is his beat."

"I'm sure he'll be here," I said. "Jews are reliable folks."

McCarthy frowned. "Cassidy ain't Jewish."

"He's a cop," I said. "Ain't all cops Jewish?"

McCarthy looked confused. "No," he said. "We're Irish. *Irish!*"

"You sure? That's not what *The Stereotype Guidebook* says."

"I'm positive." McCarthy shook his head as if trying to forget something dumb he'd just heard, then pointed at the body. "That your overcoat on the dame?"

"Any gentleman would've done that."

"That doesn't answer the question."

"Yeah, it's my fuckin' overcoat." I bent down to pick up my coat, but McCarthy shooed my hand away.

"Uh-uh," he said. "Keep your greasy gumshoe hands off. That's evidence. I gotta send that down to headquarters."

"That's *my* goddamn coat."

"You'll have to get a new one." McCarthy turned to one of the other cops, a skinny little guy who kept fondling his nightstick. "Delaney! Bag up this coat and get it over to headquarters. Have it tested for crime stuff. And, seriously, if you wanna fondle a nightstick, then fondle your own. Jesus!" He turned back to me. "I tell ya, these new recruits are just gonna be the death of me. Barely old enough to toss one back and they wanna fight crime. But I guess you'd know all about that."

"I already had this conversation with O'Riley," I said. "Don't you guys ever get tired of ridin' me?"

"Not really, no. It's funny because we don't like you."

Speaking of drinks, I needed one, and not just because I'd phoned in a murder or because this one spilled particularly gorgeous blood. In this city, that's just what makes a Thursday a Thursday. No, I needed one because I straight up couldn't function for long without a blood-alcohol level of at least oh-dot-one.

Some might call that pathological. I call it a damn fine coping strategy. Like any good strategist, I knew how to make that number add up.

"You need me for anything? O'Riley said you might have some questions."

"Did you shoot the dame?"

"No."

"Oh. Okay, well, I guess that's it. If I think of anything else, I'll let you know."

"You know where to find me."

"Yeah, I'll check the gutters."

I flagged down a cab.

"Where the fuck you think you're goin'?" McCarthy said.

"You said that was it. And that if you thought of anything else, you'd let me know."

"Well, I just thought of somethin' else."

"Shoot."

The night exploded in gunfire as Delaney drew his rod and emptied six rounds into the alley.

"Delaney, you stupid shit!" McCarthy looked as if he might have a stroke.

"The guy said shoot, so—"

"That just means ask a question! And you take orders only from me. You got that? *Me!*" McCarthy was shouting so close to Delaney's face that I thought he might take a bite out of it. "Now apologize for being stupid."

"I'm sorry for bein' stupid, sir."

"Shut up!" McCarthy turned away, looking disgusted and hopeless. "It just ain't right, Raving. They get dumber every year."

"You had a question?"

"Ah! But I forgot what it was. You'll have to come on down to headquarters and I'll ask O'Riley what I'm forgetting."

"Yeah, I dunno, Mac. I had plans to get tight down at Ariel's gin mill tonight."

"You still chasin' that dame?"

"It's for the booze," I said.

"Booze or broad, you'll have to do it a different night. Right now, you have a date with justice."

"Fine," I said. "I'll go. But only because that was a nice little turn of phrase you put together."

"Poetry comes easy to lads of the Emerald Isle," McCarthy said. "Now get in the squad car."

I spent an hour down at headquarters giving my statement and eating department doughnuts. They were better than I remembered. Murder always made me hungry and I stuffed my face while the blue coats asked me questions. I knew they were trying to pin this one on me; they were always trying to pin things on me. Murders, blackmails, those little Orphan Annie lapel pins that come in the cereal boxes. I kept denying and kept eating. Doughnuts, chips, candy bars. O'Riley let me walk out, but only after I had finished off all of the department's food and started in on the furniture. I was tired and stuffed, and decided to head back to the office for a few quick winks.

Those winks turned into a full-fledged Rip van Winkle impersonation and I woke up the next day with a powerful thirst. Police headquarters had been long on snacks but short on booze. But that's just the kind of pansies the force prefers: little wet-tittied robots who say "sir" and do what they're told. The thought made me shudder and I decided a few stiff drinks were in order. I checked my watch. 10:30. Way too late to be sober.

Ariel's was a cramped little dive a couple miles north of the Mer, on Third and Penryn, and as far as Ariel was concerned, I was a good dog. Loyal as hell, and I knew to stay off her good furniture. Wrap me around a couple bourbons, though, and I couldn't say the same for her leg. Even a good dog is still a dog.

"What'll ya have, Raving?"

Ariel's voice was honey and cigarette smoke. One of those voices that bypasses your ear entirely and hits your veins like a drug.

"The usual, Ariel," I said.

"Why, Mr. Stark Raving, do I detect the slightest hint of bullshit?"

"You know me well."

"Better than you know yourself. And even if you *could* afford the whole bar, I wouldn't sell it to you. I got other customers, you know."

I raised my hands in surrender. "Okay then, I'll just have a piece."

"Oh, darling, you couldn't afford me either," she cooed.

"Don't be cute," I said. "Okay, be cute. But do it while pouring me a drink. Scotch. Double. Neat."

When she turned to pour the scotch I could afford, I admired the property I couldn't. She was in her forties, but damn, it was a lucky man who got to share a mattress with that. Well, not her late husband, but that's another story. I intercepted the scotch before she could set it down and made half of it disappear.

"Any mail for me?"

"Just so happens, yes," she said. "It came in just a few minutes before you arrived."

"Who dropped it off?"

"Didn't see. I found it in the usual place, but whoever left it musta done it when I was busy drawin' beer." She reached under the bar and fished out an envelope. On the front, in all caps, my name. Half of being a private dick is being private, after all. I had the office for the above-bar stuff, but anything that required a bit more... discretion...I did under the table. Under the one in the back next to the Rock-Ola, to be exact.

Usually the inside of the envelopes contained jobs or cash from finished jobs. This one contained a threat.

IF YOU KNOW WHAT'S GOOD FOR YOU, YOU'LL LET THE
RATS FINISH THE JOB. STAY AWAY FROM THE ALLEY
DAME WITH THE BREAD DOUGH TITS.

On the back, in a different hand, *Thank you for your cooperation.*

"Shit, I thought this one was gonna be boring."

I put away the other half of my scotch.

Ariel leaned over the bar, bracing herself on crossed arms. The neck of her blouse fell open, revealing even more of her bread dough than she normally displayed. "What was going to be boring, hon?" she asked, looking up at me through eyelashes heavy with that black gooey stuff that dames make their eyelashes black and heavy with.

I managed to pull my attention away from her sloping loaves and back to the matter at hand, but it was hard. That made it difficult to concentrate.

"Not you, sweetheart," I said. "Not you."

"A case?"

"Looks that way. Found a naked doll over in the alley by Harry's."

"Dead?"

"As a church on Monday."

"Cops?"

"Too many."

"Why not let them handle it?"

I pushed the note across the bar. She read it.

"You shoulda seen this dame," I said.

"I've never known you to have it on for a dead one."

"She just…she just got me, ya know? Right around here." I waved my hand in the general area of my chest.

"I would've guessed a little lower," Ariel said. "Are you sure this doesn't have anything to do with—"

I interrupted her by banging my empty scotch glass on the bar. "I'll take another," I said.

"Should I leave the bottle?"

"Yeah, but don't make it so obvious."

"Anything for you, Raving honey." She moved the bottle closer. "Just think long and hard before you get into somethin' that ain't your business."

"That's the problem. I probably woulda let the blue bellies earn their keep, but this note makes me curious. Pisses me off. Nobody tells me what to do. Besides, given the trouble the killer went through to write this note, there must be more to the murder than I thought."

"Deep waters."

"It ain't easy to write a note in all caps," I said. "Lots of extra wrist movement. Means someone's pretty serious about this."

"And I'll tell ya somethin' else this means."

"What's that?"

"It means someone's watchin' you, Stark Raving."

The next morning, I sat in my office on the 16th floor of the Wilshire Building at the intersection of Third and Penryn, bottle-feeding a newborn hangover. My ad in the Yellow Pages bragged about a corner office overlooking the city, but it would've been better if I'd kept my mouth shut. It wasn't unusual to get a call from a confused client saying they had somehow passed my address and ended up at an ancient building they were sure was scheduled for demolition. The sting of admitting they were at the right place never dulled.

I leaned back in my chair and it creaked like the Mayflower in rough waters. Displaying childlike trust, I put my feet up on my desk. That desk was the one thing I was proud of in this shit storm of an office. Large, mahogany, imposing, intricately carved down each corner. You could even see some of the original finish through the scratches covering the top. I covered most of the scratches by strategically placing stacks of paper. That had the added benefit of making it look like I had a heavy caseload. Which I didn't. The papers were mostly rejected pages from the detective novel I was trying to write in my spare time. Tolstoy thought he was the only real writer in the city—and maybe he was—but I liked to pass the spare time by spinning a yarn or two. I never sent any of mine out into the world, though. Too scared. I could face a tough packing heat no problem, but ask me to send a few sheets to a goddamn paper pusher and I froze up like Betty Grable in a north wind.

I couldn't get the note from Ariel's off my mind. Like Ariel said, it wasn't my business. The cops were handling this one. Why not just do what the note said and let the whole thing slide? And it wasn't like there was any coin in it. I didn't even have a client. No one to pay expenses, to say nothing of my fee. I just couldn't get the girl out of my mind. I swear to mother fucking Christ, it wasn't just the tits. She had a grip on me. Was it the green eyes, the red lips, the pleading expression? I should've counted myself lucky I never met her while she was alive. That dame would've twisted me six ways to Sunday.

The phone rang.

"Hello. Raving Detective Agency. I'm Stark Raving."

"Well, golly gee, perhaps I'd better call someone else!" The voice had the crack of adolescence. I hated kids that age. Especially smart alecks.

"You do so at your own peril," I said.

"Gallopin' gentiles! You really *are* a loon!"

"Oh, for...for fuck's sake. That's my name! I—!"

The line went dead. One of these days, I was going to make enough money to move out to a quiet little cottage on a riverbank and—

The telephone rang. If it was that kid again, I was going to track him down and beat the pimples right off his ass. I sighed but girded my loins and answered.

"Hello. Raving Detective Agency."

"May I speak to Mr. Raving?" Finally, lady luck had dealt in my favor. It was a woman's voice. She sounded high class, spouting that faux Brit accent favored by Hollywood film stars and bluebloods from the coast.

"This is Raving."

"Ah, Mr. Raving. How good to speak to you." The dame might have been up in years, but she still knew how to draw out words like "good" and "you" so they stroked a man's vanity and made him wonder if vanity might not be a good name for his nightstick.

"Is it?"

"I enjoy speaking to men. And I'm good at it."

"I admire your confidence. Sounds like you've had a lot of practice."

The woman laughed, and in that moment, her voice sounded young. "I'm not sure if you're complimenting or insulting. I'll assume the former, as I make it a habit to believe in my daughter's judgment of character."

"Sounds like you got the wrong guy."

"Please, Mr. Raving. Hear me out."

"It's your dime."

"My daughter has been writing to me for several

weeks about you. How kind you've been to her and how you've gone out of your way to make sure she was safe and comfortable in a new city. I can't tell you how much that means to me."

"Look, lady, I—"

"But now I must confess to being just a bit worried about her. Her daily letters stopped arriving last week and I haven't received a phone call for at least that long. This isn't like her, Mr. Raving. Tell me, have you seen her recently? Is she all right?"

I had no idea what the broad was going on about and I opened my mouth to clue her in, but something—my private dick sense, the one that helps me solve crimes—stopped the words before they fell from my lips.

"Well, Mrs..."

"Oh, I'm so sorry. I completely forgot the social niceties. Gild is the name."

"Well, Mrs. Gild, I wish I could help you, but I haven't seen your daughter in…well, in a while."

"You haven't heard a thing?"

"I'm afraid not."

"Would you mind terribly coming to see me, Mr. Raving? I'd love to talk to you about Gwenny."

"Gwenny?"

"My daughter, Gwendoline. Her friends knew her as Gwen or Gwenny. But of course, you knew that."

Silence.

"So I may expect you?"

"I'm afraid my schedule—"

"I'm staying at the Garish Hotel, suite 109."

"Look, Mrs. Gild—"

"I realize you are a working man, Mr. Raving. Whatever your hourly rate is, I'll double it. Just being able to talk about Gwenny may soothe my frazzled nerves."

"I don't usually meet with clients in person."

"Please come, Mr. Raving."

Maybe it was the way she said "come," but I gave up the fight. "Alright, Mrs. Gild," I said. "I'll be over within the hour."

This whole thing smelled fishy, and if there's one member of the animal kingdom I hate as much as rats, it's fish. It's their eyes. I don't trust anything that doesn't blink. Fish always got that look on their faces like they think they're better than me. I eat them only to prove them wrong.

Something about this Gild jane told me she thought *I* was better than me, and that set off all kinds of alarms in my head. Anyone who knows me knows I'm not the type to babysit no fresh-faced tomato just for the hell of it. Someone was...whatever the opposite of dragging my name through the mud was. Some cat was washing the mud off mine.

"Oh my god. Fuck fish! Just...stab!" I spat through clenched teeth.

"What's that, pal?" said the cabbie, throwing one of his hairy mook arms over the back of the front seat for leverage so he could turn and look at me.

"Nothin'. How about you just watch the road, huh?"

"Okay, but ya still haven't told me where ya wants me to take ya."

I looked down at my slacks. About the only thing good about them was they kept the cold breeze off my getaway sticks. Goddamn things were older than this gink's cab and twice as grimy, and the slacks were almost as bad. If I was going to convince Gild I was who she thought I was, I needed to look like the guy I thought she thought I'd look like. First rule in the private dicking handbook. I needed to see a man about a suit.

"That Chinese place on Third and Penryn."

"Marcus' joint? Guy who sells them nice secondhand rags?"

"That's the one."

"You sure that's the one you're thinkin' of?"

"As shit. Dry cleaning place. Big windows fulla suits. I go there all the time. C'mon, let's blow."

"Okay, but he ain't Chinese is all," the mook said, heaving himself back toward the windshield. He put the big Plymouth in gear and nosed it into traffic.

"Of course, he is. Guy runs a dry cleaner's. That's how stereotypes work."

"Sounds like—"

He stopped there because he caught a look at my mug in his rear view mirror. If I didn't know stereotypes, I didn't know my dick from an eggroll, and I didn't need some hack driver confusing things. I tipped the lug an extra twenty cents because he kept his stupid trap shut for the rest of the trip.

I got out of the cab and walked inside Marcus' joint.

"Good afternoon, Mr. Raving! How's tricks?" Marcus said. Big fella. Big voice.

"Been better," I said. "How's business in the Orient?"

"Man, not that shit again. How many black Chinamen you ever seen, Raving? I reckon you're the most confused racist I ever met."

"I'm just tryin' to fit into my era. Besides, I consider myself an expert on stereotypes. I even have a book that details every one of 'em."

Marcus closed his eyes and took a long, deep breath. "You got a guide book on stereotypes?"

"Sure do! Carry it with me everywhere. Take me, for instance. I'm an alcoholic private detective with a shady past. According to my stereotype guide, I am…" I pulled the book from my inside jacket pocket and checked the index. "Holy shit, it says here I should be a fat bald guy who talks like an Old West prospector. Huh. That doesn't seem right."

"And you need this book because *why* exactly?"

"It helps me interact with folks who are different from me. You know how awkward *that* can be."

"I don't s'pose you could just treat everyone the same."

"I usually separate people into two main groups: those who need pastin' and those who don't." I cast a sideways glance at Marcus. "Why, someone been treatin' you bad? Tell me who it is and I'll put 'em on the list of future pastings. Maybe even give 'em a copy of this guidebook so they'll stay out of trouble in the future."

Marcus smiled and threw a mock punch in my direction. "Lucky for you, I know you got a good heart, or I'd hang one on ya."

"Good heart, eh? Ha. That's why I like you, Marcus—your prices and your lies are both top-notch."

"Chew my nightstick, Raving. Now tell me. What can I do for my favorite miserly shamus today? You lookin' to cover that old corpse 'a yours with something from this decade?"

"Yeah, somethin' like that," I said. "You think you could cram me into something swank for a double sawbuck?"

"That's Stark Raving to a T!" Marcus laughed. "Man, if air cost money, you'd breathe farts if it'd save you a couple clams."

"I prefer to rely on my sterling personality when it comes to making a good impression. It's the only part of my appearance I can't get mustard stains on."

"I hear ya. Come on over here and take a look. Got an overcoat and some slacks a chiseler about your size left here when he couldn't come up with the scratch for the cleaning. It ain't a full suit, but I think we can slap something together."

Marcus walked out from behind the counter and I followed him over to a corner of the shop where he had a rack of miscellany covered with a white sheet. I did all my shopping at his impound lot. Thriftiness is next to cleanliness, like they say, and cleanliness attracts the dames, like they say after that. The rest is just moaning. Marcus whisked the cloth off and turned to eye me. He fetched a shirt off the rack and held it up. "This one might be a little tight around the gut, but I think you can make it work if you don't breathe too deep."

"You're a riot, Marcus."

"You know you love me," he said, snatching a set of charcoal gray trousers. He handed me the clothes and turned to a shelf lined with shoes. "Either of these stompers strike your fancy?" He held up a pair of wingtips in each hand, one pair piano black, the other piano brown.

"Which pair is cheaper?"

"Christ, you're almost as stingy as that weedy little writer cat you always hangin' out with. Either pair'll run ya a clam twenty."

"I'll take one of each, then."

"And leave me with a mismatched pair? Ain't everyone got a sense of, er, *style* like you got, Raving."

"Fine. I'll take both and have a spare set. Happy? You can be pushy as a Bulgarian, you know that?"

Marcus eyeballed me. "The book again?"

I shrugged. "Hey, I didn't write it."

Marcus sighed, then handed over the shoes. I could see my map in the polished leather. Damn, I was handsome.

"You talk to the writer recently?"

"What you call him again? *Tolstoy?* Yeah, cat was in here couple days ago. Lookin' for...man, how'd he put it?

Somethin' to make him '*look like someone possessed of an entirely different physiology. Like a man who was not in fact being pursued by a motley assortment of debt collectors and underworld bruisers.*' Somethin' like that. Struck me a bit odd, but I didn't ask because I don't care."

That struck me as odd too. Tolstoy had never been particularly afraid of debt collectors before. Hell, he was basically family to them by now. Also, Marcus' impression of Tolstoy's voice was spot on, and that took me to a happy place in my head. I stepped out of my own battered stompers.

"You wanna look the other way while I slip into these duds? Don't need yer slanty eyes skatin' all over my tremendous physique," I said, unbuttoning my shirt.

"Jeee-*zus.*"

I stepped out into the noonday sun a new man. The new shirt didn't button all the way, but I was able to hide most of it behind the lavender cummerbund. The flogger was a thing to behold—a mauve and mint tartan with wide sleeves, a permanently popped collar, spacious pockets, and cover to shield my .38 from prying eyes. My own eyes were shaded by the broad brim of one helluva stovepipe hat. Goddamn *presidential.* I looked around for a cab and hailed the first one I saw. I jumped inside.

"Third and Penryn," I said, "and don't spare the horses!"

"Look, Mr. Lincoln," the cabbie said, "this ain't some dog and pony show I'm runnin' here. I'll getcha where ya need to be, but you talk civil, get me?"

"Yeah, sure," I said. Then I looked closer. "Say, aren't you that mook from the last cab ride?"

"Oh, yeah," he said. "I remember you. Decent tipper."

I wondered how I was going to explain that I was fresh out of spendies. My keen sense kicked in again and I decided not to mention my lack of funds until after the trip was over.

"Okay," the cabbie said. "This here is your stop."

I got out. "Say, how about you wait for me?"

"Yeah, I dunno, pal, that'll keep the meter runnin'. You'll run up quite a bill that way."

"It's fine. I'm here to see some rich person. I'll get them to cover it. Maybe even throw in a dollar tip."

The mook's eyes lit up at the mention of the dollar.

"You got it, pal," he said. "I'll sit here until the cows come home. Only don't make it too long. Cows get homesick, ya know."

Armed with this new and entirely useless bit of knowledge, I pivoted on my heel and walked through the opulent doors of the Garish Hotel.

I hadn't gotten more than three steps into the lobby when a kid in a red velvet coat accosted me.

"I'm sorry, sir," he said, grabbing me by the arm, "but I can't let you into th—" With fluid grace, I pivoted on my other heel and broke his grip. I pasted him one right in the puss, laying him out flat.

"What's your game, huh?" I shouted into his neck.

"You tryin' to get yourself killed?"

"Help!" he squeaked, all pitiful-like. Then I saw his nametag—Jerry Mathers—and noticed the hotel insignia on his coat. Another bird came running over, a real fancy fellow with a top hat and a black suit and cravat.

"What's the meaning of this?" he huffed. He squinted at me real unpleasant, his face all pinched up like a rabbit's ass. He helped the bellhop up.

"Fucker grabbed me," I explained, smoothing the kid's knuckle prints out of my new overcoat.

"I thought he was a bindle punk," the kid mumbled through his swollen lips.

"Your mother's a bindle punk," I shot back. "I just bought these rags! They're top'a the line, I'll have you know. Best the Orient had on offer!"

"Enough! Mathers, go clean yourself up." He turned to me. "As for you, I really must ask you to vacate these premises posthaste, sir. We expect a certain level of…refinement…from our clientele. I'm afraid that level is still quite out of rea—"

With fluid grace, I pivoted on one heel, then back again on the other, and pasted the bird in the puss. I tossed one of my cards onto his groin, stepped over him, and strolled out of the lobby all casual-like. Racism is one thing, but classism chafed my sack something fierce, and it did my soul good to paste it out of folks on occasion. I may have even tipped my swell new hat to a couple of lookers in evening gowns, because I was feeling pretty white.

Suite 109, the Gild dame had said. I figured this would be pretty easy for a right gumshoe like myself, and the doors were numbered. Duck soup. But the first one in the hall was 100. What became of 1 through 99?

"I swear to Sinatra, if I find the low-down redhot who made off with a quarter of this building, I'll paste his puss so hard...!" I roared. I balled up my pasters and swung a couple practice pastes.

"This hallway *could* use a touch more justice," said a voice. A female one, and one that sounded familiar. A bit old, but refined, like it was dipped in caviar and covered with nickels. I pivoted sharply on both heels. She stood, one hand on the knob of her suite door, the other on her hip. Both were covered in black gloves, gold bands, and strings of marbles all the way up to her elbows. Her hips were covered in sapphires. That was one expensive dress, and it complemented the slim, angular figure it was draped over like booze complements more booze.

"Mrs. Gild, I presume," I said. I pivoted forward quickly and closed the distance.

"Yes," she murmured, inspecting me from head to toe. "Mr. Raving, I likewise presume?"

"In the shoes," I said, following her gaze. My shoes were the part of this outfit I was most proud of. Ace pivoters, and shiny as hell to boot.

"The brown one's for ass-kickin'."

"They are splendid shoes, Mr. Raving," she said.

Her lips were 'sticked a familiar cherry red, and she'd colored her upper eyelids a mint green with a dusting of some kind of dense pigmented powder. "Won't you come in?"

Great throbbing nightstick of Zeus, this was a ritzy joint. It made the rooms at the Mer look like outhouses. I'd never seen a hotel room with its own servants' quarters. The entire ceiling was chandeliers, and every piece of the red leather-bound furniture was so polished I could see my ass in it before I sat down.

"I can't tell you how much I've been waiting for this," I said, dropping into an armchair. I immediately slid out and fell to the floor with an undignified thump. Goddamn things were *slick.*

"As have I, Mr. Raving!" said Mrs. Gild, seating herself gingerly in the chair facing mine. "It's good to finally meet face to face the man I've heard so much about."

"I meant sitting down," I said. I carefully angled my backside parallel with the cushion before gently lowering myself. "My dogs are killin' me."

"Oh?"

"Yes, ma'am. Lots of pivoting today. It's rough on the heels."

"Ma'am, even! Please, call me Laura. Or Lollipop, like my girlfriends do. Oh, but where are my manners? Can I offer you something to drink? Scotch? Whiskey? Rum? Gin? Brandy? Vodka? Cognac? Tequila? Absinthe?"

"Yes."

"Which one?"

"Yes."

"Perhaps you'd like to serve yourself? The bar is behind you. It covers the whole east wall, so it's hard to miss."

I pivoted on my ass.

"Perhaps I would," I said, miraculously still able to speak. I'm not ashamed to admit that I was hard as diamonds at that point. I covered my erection with my hat and penguin-walked briskly behind the bar.

"I must say, you're every bit as charming as Gwenny's letters made you out to be," Laura said. "A bit more, shall we say, sturdily built and colorfully dressed than I expected, though." She plucked a silver picture frame off the end table next to her chair. "Still, a gorgeous girl like her would do well to have at her disposal a man who can handle himself in a fight. Lord knows she's melted the heart of more than one poor sap who wouldn't take no for an answer."

She held the picture out so I could see it.

Just as I'd had no reason to suspect but did anyhow—the tomato in the photograph was the same tomato in the alley, no mistake. I am a little ashamed to admit I was glad I had the bar between Gild's eyes and my groin. Gwen was a dish all right, and even in the two dimensions, her green eyes cut right through me.

I needed to get my mitts on those letters. Not knowing my own goddamn backstory was making me uncomfortable. But first, I had to break some bad news to this poor dame.

I gulped down a hooker of brandy to brace myself. Then I gulped down a hooker of whiskey. Then one of absinthe. And another of brandy. Then I tucked a bottle of gin into my coat pocket.

"Ma'am. Laura. Mrs. Lollipop Gild. I'm afraid I got some bad news for you." I took off my hat and placed it back on my head. Then I removed it and held it against my chest all somber-like.

"You're out of gin."

"Why, that's not a problem at all. I have—"

"And your daughter is dead."

She sprang to her feet faster than I thought someone of her age and regal bearing could manage. Against that slippery goddamn leather too. Broad must've had an ass like a pair of golf cleats covered in sandpaper.

"How dare you joke about such a thing!"

"I'm afraid I ain't just pullin' yer pin, ma'am," I said. "I'm a private dick, and we don't joke about that kinda thing. She took a slug right to the tit, croaked her instantly. So, well, it ain't like she suffered."

She looked like she wanted to hurl that picture frame right into my mug, her own a tangle of anguish and fury. But there was something else there too: resignation. Crazy as it sounds, I don't think she was entirely surprised by my news.

Then all the fight just went outta her.

"Oh, god," she said, sinking back into her chair. She adhered to the edge of the seat and buried her face in her hands, all forty-five pounds of bracelets clanking and jangling with her sobs. I went to her, then back to the bar for another hooker of brandy, then back to her again. I lay a hand on her back.

"Laura," I said, kinda quiet, "I may not be the angel in Gwenny's letters—in fact, I know I ain't—but I'll find the bindlefucks who did this and put 'em six feet under. You have my word. And my invoice. If you accept."

She looked up at me, her eyelash-weighting goo smeared and running down her cheeks like jilted rain on the street of a lover.

"I accept," she said in a whisper. "But on one condition: you keep the police force out of it. You promise me that, Mr. Raving, and you will be a wealthy man."

I liked the sound of that.

"Wealth I can do," I said. "But just one more thing. Would you mind if I took a look at Gwen's letters? Her death is kinda hittin' me hard, as you might expect, and I think the letters might, ya know, give me closure."

"Oh, of course, Mr. Raving. Wait here." She left the room and returned with a packet of letters held together with a rubber band. "You can take them with you, in fact. I know she'd want you to have them."

I felt kinda bad about the deception but not bad enough, and I beat it out of there before she could change her mind.

Even with all of the recent drinking, my throat was dry as Hepburn's snatch, but I resisted the urge to head over to Ariel's. Something was poking at my brain fat, something that had been bothering me. It was that little rat of a friend of mine, Tolstoy, and how he'd reacted to seeing the body. Sure, it could tweak a guy's nips to catch sight of a gorgeous doll, dead and cold, but it had seemed like more than that. Tolstoy had been all over seeing the body earlier. But once he'd seen her face, he went all limp—almost like he'd recognized her. Yes, Ariel's would have to wait. Besides, I could drink that bottle of gin from Laura's hotel room on the way. The cabbie was still waiting for me and I realized I'd forgotten to ask Laura for money.

"Well, shit," I said.

"That don't sound good," the mook said. "That sounds like some chiseler comin' up with a reason he don't got money."

"You're a very insightful fellow." I waved the bottle of gin at him. "This is good stuff, real top shelf hooch. I'll share it with you. The bottle probably costs more than your cab."

The mook grabbed the bottle, opened it, and glugged down a good quarter of the contents. He made a gargling sound, swished it around his mouth, swallowed, and grinned. I wondered if his teeth had been in that condition prior to guzzling all that gin.

"Yeah, that's good stuff," he said. "Lots better'n that swill my brudder makes in his bathtub."

"Sounds awful."

"Aw, wouldn't be so bad if they didn't use it to wash up on the weekend. Last time I drank a bottle of his, I spent all night pickin' pubes outta my teeth."

By the time the cab pulled up in front of the Mer, we had finished the bottle and started on the seventeenth chorus of "Mother Machree." The cab didn't so much pull up as it did drive over the curb and mow down a fireplug.

"Well, ain't this a thing," the mook said, his voice thick with booze. "Sun's out and shinin' and it's rainin'! We must be sittin' under a cloud!"

"I think we ran over a plug," I said. My words sounded funny, but I felt very clever. "I'll get out and check." I opened the door and sorta ejected myself from the cab. I landed on the sidewalk on all fours and scuffed the knees of my new pants.

I looked back to thank the cabbie, but he was staring down the street, his face displaying the focus and determination of a man trying to thread an invisible needle. He threw the Plymouth into gear. The beast roared like a steel buffalo in heat and shot off down the sidewalk, taking out benches and trashcans like he was getting paid for it. I heard him launch into the eighteenth chorus of "Machree" and watched him go, his path of destruction growing smaller with distance, his terrible singing voice fading away. Then I started crawling toward the front door of the Mer.

By the time I reached Tolstoy's door, I had managed to stagger upright, but it was still a shaky proposition. I knocked on the door, not out of any sense of propriety, but because I wanted another minute to gather my thoughts. The gin and the parade of drinks I'd had at

Gild's were starting to kick in. I prided myself on my capacity for liquor, but this was hitting me hard.

"Well, you're a drunk one," Tolstoy said, opening the door.

"Got some crackers?" I stumbled into the room. "I could use some crackers. Soak up some of this booze."

"Check the cupboard. Listen, Stark, I have a new screenplay I wanted to run by you. I think it might be a good one."

It might have been the booze, but it seemed to me that Tolstoy was behaving a little more like a rat than usual. All twitchy and nervous, eyes darting around, his hands either fiddling with the buttons on his shirt or turning that ugly hat of his over and over.

"I can't fuckin' read a screenplay right now," I said. "I can't even read the words on this cracker box. The crackers taste alright, though."

"Those aren't crackers, those are jazz records. Stop eating my Dizzy Gillespie."

"Ah, I thought they were a little big and stale."

"Stark, this is important."

"So's my stomach. All this booze is eating a hole in my tummy and your crackers taste like trumpets. Ugh. I bet it was the absinthe. There's a reason that stuff is illegal."

"Fine," Tolstoy said. "You just keep dining upon my records and I will read my screenplay to you." He cleared his throat. "FADE IN: A detective discovers a naked woman dead in the alley—"

"Look, I'm sure your play is fuckin' tops. But I'm really getting a headache. How about I take a little snooze on your couch and you can read me the whole fuckin' thing when I wake up."

"You don't understand," Tolstoy said. "I need—"

A knock on the door interrupted him. We both looked around and saw Miss Foxie poke her head inside.

"Phone call for you, Mr. Tolstoy."

Again, it could have been the booze, but I swear I saw Tolstoy's face go a little paler than usual. Sweat popped out on his forehead and upper lip.

"W-w-who is it?"

"Fella wouldn't say his name. Just said to get you on the phone or, and I quote, he would skin you alive and use your hide as a bedsheet."

"Excuse me," Tolstoy said to me. "This sounds like an important phone call. Don't leave!"

I followed him into the hall. I was drunk all right, but now it felt like my goddamn legs were trying to walk off by themselves.

"If I stay, do I have to listen to your screenplay? Not that I ain't supportive, you understand. Hell, I think your stuff is better than most of that bilge down at the theater. But my head is really—"

He wasn't listening to me. Instead, he had the phone's earpiece pressed tightly to his ear and was muttering into the mic. I cocked my head to listen.

"I'll have it," Tolstoy said. "I said I'd have it early next month. I—no—no, sir...I realize that...no, I wouldn't even think of…just give me a few more days…I can't—well—no, it's not—" He stopped talking and took the handset from his ear hole. He just stood there, looking at it like he'd never seen such a thing before. Then he put it back on its cradle and gave it the look of a man both disgusted and scared shitless.

"Hey, you all right?" A chorus of warning bells joined the rest of the clanging in my head. I moved forward and gripped Tolstoy's shoulder. He didn't seem to notice. "You all right?"

He moved away from me, back toward his room. "Listen, Stark. You—you need to read this screenplay. Maybe just the first scene. Read it while I'm gone, okay?"

"While you're gone? You can't go anywhere; you look like a ghost's ghost. You're whiter than Wendell Willkie."

He weaseled out of my grip. "I have to go."

I made a grab for him, but he easily evaded me. As he scurried all rat-like down the hall, he yelled over his shoulder, "Just fucking read it!"

I watched him go, swayed a little, and then moved back to the room. *I'll show him what I think of his fucking screenplay.* I grabbed the pages and dropped them into the trash and then dropped myself onto the couch and passed out.

When I woke up, I wished I hadn't. Tolstoy's apartment was way too goddamned bright, like he'd opened all the windows he didn't have and replaced all his burned out bulbs and turned them on. I slammed my eyes shut and tried to sit up.

"Whoa, easy there, murderer," said a voice. It wasn't Tolstoy's, but I wasn't so curious I was gonna open my eyes.

"Who the—?" Then it hit me. It was that mook cab driver! What the hell was he doing in Tolstoy's place?

"Yeah, you tried to do me in with some poisoned gin, bub. Not kosher. I had a lotta assholes try to get out of feedin' the meter before, but nobody ever tried to bump me off with booze. Gotta say, I kinda like your style."

"The hell are you on about?" I muttered. I still had my eyes shut, and I started feeling all around with my hand. Sheets. Bed. Rail on the side of the bed. This wasn't Tolstoy's moldy old couch.

"Where am I?"

"We're at St. Gregory's Hospital," said the mook. He sounded happy about it, like he didn't get a chance to go inside a lot of buildings with electricity and plumbing and shit. Like this was a field trip to him.

"Okay. Now tell me why the fuck we're in a hospital."

"Poison!" he hooted. "You tried to off me with that bottle of Nevada gas." If I ever got my eyes working again, I was going to find him and paste that stupid grin right off his face. He was enjoying this.

"No no no," I said. I opened one eye experimentally. The blinding white room was starting to dim a bit, and I could see it was more of a shade of sad wintergreen. The institutional color of boredom and measles. "No," I reaffirmed. "If I was gonna rub you out, you'd know about it, because you'd be dead. And I'd know about it because I'd be missing a bullet. And why in the name of St. Gregory's gangrenous cockshaft would I bother trying to off you? I'm basically traveling on credit with you, and not a lotta cabbies give a fella that kinda leeway."

"I am pretty great," admitted the mook. "Good thing you was a greedy sumbitch and drank most of it yourself. So what was you doin' suckin' on a bottle of poisoned gin anyway?"

That was a damn good question. Before I could answer, a tall blonde guy in a white coat shoved aside the curtain around my bed and dropped a clipboard on my shins.

"Oh, I see you're awake, Mr. Raving," he said all slow and laconic, like he thought he was better than me because he hadn't been poisoned. "For a while, I didn't think you were going to make it."

"Too many hoods need pastin'," I said. "And some doctors."

"Well, you're a lucky man," he said, looking at some papers. "The amount of cyanide you ingested would have killed a party of eight Neanderthals *and* the mastodon they were hunting. I honestly don't know how you survived."

"Practice."

"I survived too!" piped up the mook.

I grabbed the doc's arm. "How long have I been out?"

"Oh, I don't know," the doc said. "I've never been than good with time. A day or more…I really couldn't say. Hell, I don't even know what year it is."

"A day?"

"Or more."

I sat up in the bed and shook my head in an effort to see straight.

"I gotta get out of here," I said. "I have people depending on me."

"That's what they keep telling me too." The doc looked around the room, as if looking for someone to tell him what to do next. "You're both free to go, I suppose."

And then he just walked out. Didn't even take his clipboard.

"You're driving," I told the mook. "I'm pretty sure I know who tried to kill me, and I plan to deal with that in due time, but I gotta get back to the Mer, and fast. Buddy of mine's in trouble."

"To Third and Penryn!"

The mook dropped me back off at Tolstoy's place. Tolstoy himself was nowhere to be found. It was oddly still in the apartment without the fucking tapping of his typewriter assaulting my earholes. My head pounded. I needed a drink of water or, better yet, a good slug of that fucking dog's hair.

Strange that Tolstoy was still out. As far as I knew, I was his only friend. He didn't bar hop. He didn't have a job. He ordered most of his meals in from Harry's. A feeling of unease stole over me like the someone just uncorked a bottle of cheap farts across the room. Where *was* that little fuck? And then it hit me like a barrel full of dicks, the obvious thing that the curtain of cyanide had so capably concealed. Tolstoy was a needy little shit and loved to foist his scribbles on others, but he wasn't *that* needy.

I scrambled to the wastebasket and pulled out the handful of typed pages I'd thrown away just prior to collapsing on the couch. There must be something in the scene that Tolstoy wanted me to read. My eyes scanned the pages, reading as fast as the old mug marbles would go. The quality of the writing...wasn't. For all his many rat-like faults, the little shit was a pretty darn good inkslapper and this stuff wasn't up to his usual standard. Which confirmed my suspicion that he had written it with a certain purpose in mind. The final nail in the coffin of my doubts was nailed in early in the first scene, when a detective named Rark Staving found the body of a dead woman in the alley between the Sea Hotel and Baldy's

Saloon. The little fuck knew my weakness for dumb jokes. That sort of humor always tickled me right in the happy sack. But I knew now wasn't the time for happy sack tickling, especially in scene two, when I found out that Staving's tiny friend, Chekhov, had known the stiff. The screenplay ended mid-sentence halfway through scene two, just after I learned that Chekhov was in danger somehow. It was just like that asshole to leave it at a cliffhanger. I made a mental note to paste his puss for that the next time I saw him.

Danger, huh? That would explain the mysterious phone call and Chek—er—Tolstoy's disappearance. I folded up the pages of the screenplay and shoved them into my inside jacket pocket. These were going down the throat of somebody. Either Tolstoy or whoever made off with him. I was pissed and somebody was going to get beaned for it. I had a fucking nasty hangover, my head was busting, redhot pokers were stabbing my brain, and I was in a spectacularly bad mood. Tolstoy was a shitty friend, but he was *my* shitty friend. So help me if they hurt that little sonofabitch—

I beat it to the check-in desk and cornered Miss Foxie, who was leaning back in her chair smoking a cigarette. Her feet were propped up on the desk and I could see all the way up to the Promised Land. She also had a tit hanging out for no reason whatsoever.

"What's up, big boy," she mewed. "Is it what I hope it is?"

"Later, sweetheart. I have some queries about

Tolstoy."

"What about him?"

"When did he leave?"

"Maybe a day ago. Seemed to be in a hurry. Kept checkin' his watch."

"Was he alone?"

"Yeah, he was alone. But no aloner than me. You sure you don't want to have a little fun?" She flexed her chest muscles, making her exposed tit bounce gruesomely.

"Put away the baked good, Foxie."

"What, one ain't good enough? You want 'em both?"

"Two terrible things don't cancel each other out," I said. "Listen, toots, this is important."

She pouted but popped the runaway loaf back inside. "I dunno anything about Tolstoy. He left in a hurry, that's all I know."

"Maybe you're feedin' me a line."

"Maybe I am. Maybe I'm not. Maybe you should be nicer to dames like me, what only wants a little company." She continued pouting, but she was bad at it. Her lower lip stuck out like a locomotive cow-catcher and was just as attractive.

"Maybe I should paste you around a little."

"You'd never hit a woman."

"No," I said, "but what does that have to do with you?" It was a low blow, but I was mad because she had me. I could never lay out a dame, not having seen what I'd seen.

Foxie stretched out in her chair and peered at me through squinty, calculating, lustful eyes. "Tell you what, handsome, I'll bargain a future roll in the hay against my promise to let you know if I hear anything. You game?"

I sighed. "Fuck it. Fine. But it has to be useful information."

"I'm always useful, baby."

"Can you at least tell me what direction he went outta here?"

"I think he turned right. Towards Harry's."

"Thanks."

"Does that count as useful information?"

"No! We haven't started yet."

I scooted outside before she had a chance to start up that gruesome pout again. There wasn't much in the direction of Harry's Bar. This was the southern edge of town, the disreputable zone where folks didn't go unless they were down on their luck or looking for trouble. A homeless guy loitered on the street corner, hitting up the few passing cars and keeping his eyes peeled for cops. I recognized him, so I walked over and handed him a nickel.

"Many thanks, my good man," he said.

"That ain't a gift, Roger. I'm looking for information."

"Any insights I may be able to provide will be my pleasure, I assure you," Roger said. Roger had been a classical actor back in the day, but the day had disappeared in a cloud of reefer smoke and a few harder drugs that sapped his mind and made him impossible to work with. He had appeared in several films and worked with Orson Welles on a production of *Macbeth*. But the drug use eventually made him a studio liability and now he was a Hollywood persona non grata.

"You seen Tolstoy lately?"

"Ah, the writer!"

I nodded.

"Quite. I observed the man running from the Mer and heading for Harry's."

"He went to Harry's?"

"No, but he tried to. He had almost reached the door when a black car pulled up. The door opened and two men got out."

"Well, what happened?"

"They began addressing Tolstoy, who became agitated."

"Agitated?"

"Waving his arms about and speaking in a raised voice. The usual."

"Could you make anything out?"

"Just a few words."

"Try to remember."

"Oh, something about this being between them only, and how they should leave everyone else alone."

"Anything else?"

"They finally tired of his antics and one of the men struck Tolstoy in the face."

"Pasted his puss, huh?"

"If you say so."

This made me mad. Nobody went around pasting

pusses but me.

Roger continued, "Then they grabbed his arms and tossed him into the back of the car."

"What kind of car?"

"I'm afraid I don't know my vehicles. Large car, black. One like the studio heads drive. Expensive."

My growing family of hangovers, cyanide-shredded insides, and headful of shitty memories needed a drink, a good stiff one like the kind Ariel mixed up just for me. A brief ten-minute calculation, and I worked out where to get one. *Ariel's bar.*

When I walked in, she was just switching out the gin bottles. That gave me an even better idea.

"Save yourself some elbow grease," I said, "and just slide that new bottle my way. I'll mix my own drink: gin mixed with my face." She obliged. I filled a glass and emptied it again.

"You look like holy fuck," Ariel said.

"I feel worse. I feel like Satan's taint went on a field trip to a buzz saw convention."

"I was going to say you looked like Satan's taint, but it seemed a little harsh. You must have a hangover."

"Worse. Hangovers I can handle. This was something we in the gumshoe trade like to call 'some fuckwit broad tried to kill me by lacing her booze with cyanide and letting me steal it'."

"Oh my god! Who? I'll shank the bitch!"

"You're not gonna believe this, but remember the

dead alley dame from a few days ago?"

"I do, because *my* brain isn't pickled."

I ignored that.

"Get this; it was the alley dame's *mother!* Said her name was Gild. Brought me on to investigate the whole sorry affair. But here's what don't make sense to me. Why would she go through the trouble of hirin' me before bumpin' me off? Dingbat needs a new hobby."

"Or the poison was meant for her."

"Shit, if she was gonna poison herself, she didn't need to invite me over to watch."

"No, I mean someone's tryin' to bump *her* off!"

I hated it when people did my job better than me. I chalked it up to having just recently given Death the finger. That kinda of thing tends to take a bit of the moxie out of a fella. On the other hand, these dames could just be covering for each other. Not that Ariel would play me for a fool, but women tended to see the best in themselves and the worst in men. Of course, that may just be because men are the worst.

"You know the only cure for cyanide booze?" Ariel said.

"Non-cyanide booze?"

"Exactly." She grabbed the bottle out of my hand, took a swig, and handed it back. "So you just pissed off about the poisoning or is there somethin' else eating your dick."

"It's Tolstoy."

"That little rat?"

"He's pretty awful, ain't he? But he's missing. And according to Roger the Homeless Actor, he was last seen with two big fuckers who made a good show of kidnapping him."

"Who would kidnap Tolstoy?"

"That's what I'd like to know. There's a decent chance they'll get sick of his wheezing and puns and let him loose, but they also might kill him. That's the choice I'm faced with most of the time. The only reason I haven't killed him so far is because I don't have another poker partner lined up."

"You could play with me."

"I thought we'd burned that bridge."

"No, I mean cards."

I took a drink. The thought of playing cards with Ariel brought up bad memories. Memories of an era that took place before the present: the past. The past is where memories live, because you can't remember the future no matter how hard you try or how loud you yell.

When I didn't speak, she gave me a soft smile.

"Still hurts?" she said.

"I ain't so good with memories," I said. "Never really got the hang of 'em."

Ariel poured a shot of sadness into her smile. Her mouth still turned up at the corners, but her eyes changed. I'm sure it was pity, and normally I'd have something shitty to say if I caught someone pitying me, but not Ariel. She was the only one I'd take it from.

"Surely there are SOME good ones," she said quietly.

She put her hand on my forearm and I twisted it away.

"Probably. I mean, yeah, sure. Fuck. Balls. Look, I can't do this right now. Maybe after I get my weedy little friend back, you and I can shoot the shit over a hooker, okay?"

"Like you don't talk to enough hookers in your line of work," she said.

I grinned. Yeah, that was the Ariel I needed right now. The sassy one. I didn't need comforting. I had all the comfort I needed in this bottle of gin.

"So whaddya doin' in here soaking up all my booze, then? I got towels can do that just as well as you, and they don't piss all over the bathroom floor when they're done."

"*One* time..!"

"Twice. My point is, you ain't doin' Tolstoy any good sittin' here on your ass. You ain't doin' your ass no good either. That's Fartin' Frank's usual stool."

"Jesus."

"Don't go whinin' to him. You got work to do. Now get off your ass and get at it."

"Just one more drink."

She swiped the gin bottle with the speed of a striking viper. "Nope. I'm cuttin' you off. It's time to go find your friend."

That was all well and good for Ariel to say, what with her tits and womanly ways, but I was the one who had to do the work. And I had to admit that I had no idea where to begin. I dragged myself down to the corner to a phone booth and put in a call to the police station. I'd hoped they'd heard something, some underworld rumblings, but nothing doing. At least, nothing they were willing to tell me. Of course, I wasn't on the good boy list with the cops these days, hadn't been for a while. I'd been one of them, back when I was a greenhorn and so wet behind the ears that I'd just about drown in my hat. When I got wise and started standing up to the system, they shucked me faster than a fat guy's cob at an Iowa corn eating contest. That figure of speech made me feel sickly for some reason and I promised myself I'd never use it again. The cops knew what I thought of them. And it pissed them off. We had a tempestuous relationship, me and the cops. Like a pro skirt and her john, we found each other useful but didn't trust the other enough to really confide. If they knew anything about Tolstoy, they were playing it close to the vest.

If phone booths had pusses, I would've I pasted it for being useless. The hands of Father Time were ticking and the old bastard wasn't one for doing me favors. For all I knew, Tolstoy was being hung up to bleed somewhere, his little rat life draining away. It wasn't like me to be so dramatic, but the thought of Tolstoy turning stiff made me twitchy. I decided I didn't like that figure of speech either and crossed it off my mental list. Emotional distress always made me come up with unsettling idioms. It also gave me indigestion. Feelings. I hated feelings, what with their pointy edges making me remember that I was a man, not a machine. I preferred to be a machine.

Nothing touched me. It was better that way.

I was considering heading back to Ariel's and weaseling another drink out of her, when I heard the roar of an engine and the squeal of rubber. I turned away from the phone booth. A car, black and long and expensive-looking, had pulled up at the curb. The doors flew open and a couple goons rolled out and came for me. I could tell they weren't there selling encyclopedias. From the vacant look in their eyes, neither of them had ever cracked a book, much less figured out how to decipher those funny little black marks on the pages.

I sized them up. The one on the right looked to be a roundheel and the other was just a total sap. I figured to lay out the first and cave the other by virtue of footwork. My plan would've worked too, if I hadn't done all that recent pivoting. I gave the lead actor a good round of chin music and he backed away to shake off the tunes. I tried to duck under the sap, but my ankle gave up the ghost and I fell right into the guy's fist. Then the sidewalk got into the act and came up and gave me a lick. I decided to cheat and grabbed for my heater, but the mug was wise and planted his giant flat foot down on my wrist. The .38 skittered off the curb and fuck my tits if it didn't slide right down the storm drain. The guy I'd slugged had quieted the band and lumbered over to join his partner in beating the shit out of me. I rolled to avoid a vicious kick and clunked my bean on the edge of the phone booth for the effort. Somehow I got my feet under my fat ass and lurched upright, just in time to register a clock on the ear hole. It threw me back, but I stayed on my dogs and ducked around the side of the phone booth. Fortunately, my antagonists were dumb and it took them a minute to figure out which of them should go around which way, so I was able to catch my breath. Finally, the one I'd hit lost patience and hauled out a .45.

"Okay, dat's it!" he roared. "I'm gonna just put ya under, ya little—"

The roar of a car engine interrupted him and we all looked around to see a Plymouth charging down the street. Its horn blared and its massive grille pointed right at us. I jumped aside just in time to avoid becoming a hood ornament and the Plymouth mowed down the phone booth like it was made of matchsticks.

The lugs stood there looking at the Plymouth in disbelief but were galvanized into action when the mook cabbie jumped from the car and charged them, hairy fists flying and mook mouth insulting their mothers and sisters. The mook wasn't a particularly skilled fighter, but what he lacked in technique, he more than made up for in enthusiasm. His pasters were everywhere at once and, before long, the two lugs were beating a retreat. They popped into their big black car, locked the doors behind them, and tore off down the street.

"Let's follow those bastards!" I yelled, making for the cab.

"You nuts, pal? I just got rid of 'em!"

"Yeah, they're afraid of you now," I said. "And I'm pretty sure they know something about Tolstoy."

"You sure this little guy is worth all this trouble?"

"Not in the least. For all I know, he murdered the alley dame and set me up for it. But I can't quite believe that. And if it is true, I wanna paste 'im myself. Either way, I gotta find him."

"Aw, you're a good friend."

"Bite me," I said, throwing open the passenger door, throwing a paper-wrapped package on the seat out onto the pavement and throwing myself into the Plymouth.

"My hoagie!"

"You can bite that later!" I said, throwing him an obscene gesture.

"But the pigeons'll—"

"Fuck the pigeons!"

"Just like that? Without romancin' 'em first?"

"Just drive, willya? I'll buy you eight hoagies when we're through!"

That did it. The mook grinned, lumbered around to his door, and lumbered the key into the ignition. The big engine lumbered to life, and the Plymouth lumbered into pursuit ahead of a big cloud of blue smoke.

"Had to replace my bumper, ya know," he lumbered. "Wanna know what with?"

"No."

"Lumber!" He snort-giggled. "Big ol' log."

"Christ."

"If he's listenin', tell him thanks. I think that's yer pigeons up ahead."

I followed the mook's chubby kielbasa finger and, sure

enough, the big black car was idling at a red light at the corner of Third and Penryn. I would have thanked God for this fortunate turn of events, but I couldn't believe in a God who would make such a stupid couple of guys.

"You'd think the way they tore ass outta here, they'd just blow the light," said the mook. "There ain't even nobody in the intersection."

"Let's give 'em some encouragement."

I scooted over and planted my pivoter on top of the mook's accelerator foot. The Plymouth, already near its limit at thirty-five mph, lurched forward. The scenery outside the windows blurred as we picked up speed. Thundering along at the ragged edge of forty goddamn miles per hour, we plowed into the back of the black car. We hit low, driving the big sedan's ass end up off the pavement and sending it pirouetting across Penryn like a sozzled ballet dancer. For a couple of dumb onions, the lug and his buddy reacted quick, though. A screech of hot rubber, and they were off.

"We got 'em now!" I shouted. The impact had mashed their chrome monstrosity of a bumper into one of its rear tires. "Keep on 'em!"

"Okay, but just so's you know, you owes me a new log," said the mook, shaking an admonishing kielbasa at me.

I agreed or told him to suck a lemon or something and reached for my roscoe. Holster empty. Fuck. That's right, it was at the bottom of a sewer pipe somewhere, getting humped by rats.

"New plan. Pull alongside 'em and I'll paste the driver," I said, winding down the window. The mook obliged. The driver, the big guy, was staring straight ahead, teeth gritted. Real intense. I motioned for him to roll down his window.

"Roll down your goddamn window!" I clarified. The little guy next to him was futzing around with something I couldn't see, and the big guy had his hands full keeping the sedan pointed straight. That fucked-up rear tire was making the thing dance all over the road, spitting chunks of rubber and acrid smoke. When the lug flipped me the bird, I took a swing at the window but missed as they lurched out of my pasting range. The mook grunted something about pimento loaf and swung the Plymouth into oncoming traffic, around a couple Fords at a stop sign. He was good. If we survived this, I'd probably see my way to paying him.

The crooks had opted to rumble over the curb to avoid the Fords, and that zotzed the bum tire for good. It let go with a bang like the goddamn Fourth of July.

"They're shootin' at us!" howled the mook. He hit the brakes and the sedan, shitting sparks, roared ahead.

"No no no! They blew a tire! Keep going! They're done for now!" I was going to stomp his foot myself, but yeah, he knew the drill.

Ahead, the little guy leaned out of his window, and now I saw what he'd been fondling in his lap. It was worse than it sounded like.

"Get down!" I shouted. I shoved the mook's head

below the dash and followed suit. The weasel peppered the cab with tight-pattern buck, and the windshield exploded in a festive shower of glass, like a chandelier throwing up.

"The tire's shooting at us!" the mook mumbled. He was steering with his teeth, biting down on the bottom of the wheel like a hairy alligator.

I hazarded a glance above the cowl in time to see the weasel pump another shell into his Remington. His next shot hit the log bumper and sent a spray of woodchips in through the windshield hole. Searing pain above my right eye. A curtain of red. Shit, there went my depth perception.

His third shot caught the Plymouth right in the radiator, and that was it for us. A hiss like a thousand pissed off raccoons and we lost our prey in a cloud of Beelzebub's sauna steam. The mook face-steered us over to the side of the road, and the big engine shuddered to a halt.

"God*dammit!*" I tore open the door and tore out of the car in a half-blind rage. I tore off my flogger and mashed it over the bleeding right side of my map. Stung like a sonuvabitch where the log shrapnel'd tore it up. Out of my left eye, I saw the sedan tear ass around the corner onto Third and disappear.

"Sorry about that, pal," the mook said. "We're dead in the water."

"Fuck! I had some questions for those two," I said, clenching and unclenching my pasters.

"Yeah, well, I'm gonna need a new log," the mook said. "So you ain't the only one what's got problems."

"I need to get over to the Garish Hotel," I said. "You have any cabbie friends who might be able to pick me up?"

"Of course I got friends, but they don't like comin' over to this side of town. Kinda beneath 'em, ya know."

"Yeah, I know. So, what? I gotta hoof my way over there? It's way over on Third and Penryn! Besides, my dogs are barkin' like a hound in heat."

I looked around, but it was pretty deserted. No bus stops or waiting cabs. Not even a phone booth in sight. Then I saw something: a bicycle leaning up against the big plate glass window of a storefront. Fuck me if two things didn't awake in me at that moment: a good idea and a long buried and neglected dream of mine. I'd always wanted a bike with a nanner seat and handlebar tassels, but ma said it weren't fitting for a...well, anyway, it would be a damn sight faster than walking.

The place was a used bookstore, and when I glanced inside, I saw a little ratty kid pawing over the comics. He was the only customer, so this was probably his bike. I kept an eye on him as I sidled over and grabbed hold of the handlebars.

"You stealin' a kid's bike?" the mook said. "That's pretty low, pal."

"My pivots are pretty low. Once I'm outta sight, tell him I'll leave his wheels at the Garish Hotel. He can pick it up there. And I'll send a tow truck for your Plymouth."

I hopped on the bike and began pedaling away. The

seat was way too low and my knees kept banging into the handlebars, but it was better than walking. The kid saw me start off and came charging out of the store like he'd just seen someone stealing his bike.

"Hey, ya moron! Gimme back my Schwinn!"

I hadn't generated a good head of steam and the kid was able to catch up. He was a fast motherfucker. He ran alongside and started beating me around the head with a comic book.

"Get offa my bike!"

I glanced over my shoulder and saw the storeowner run onto the sidewalk.

"You get back here with my comic book, you little rotten shit!" He charged after us, waving a broom. He was an older guy but just as fast as the kid. "This is the last time you steal books from my shop!" He started whacking the kid's head with the bristly end of the broom.

"Ow, stop it!" the kid yelled. "And you, gimme my bike!"

I kept pedaling and the two others kept running behind me. We traveled down the sidewalk like an abusive parade. I saw a hill ahead and knew this was my chance to outpace the crazy train. As we hit the decline, I leaned into the pedals and was off like rocket, leaving the kid and the storeowner to fight it out.

Once I got up to speed, it didn't take that long to get over to the Garish. My legs were rubbery from all that pedaling, but my anger at Laura Gild, which had been rising all throughout the trip, gave me the strength to find her room, confusing number scheme be damned. I knocked on the door and when she answered, I didn't wait to be invited in. I pushed past her and strode into the room, carefully avoiding the slippery furniture. I didn't need to look like a dope right now. Instead, I moved behind the bar and bled on it.

"Mr. Raving, what a pleasure! But oh, my god, what happened to your face?"

"Shut up, ya crazy dame, and start talkin'."

"I beg your pardon?"

"You know what I mean. The poison. Did you really think you could bump me off with a little whizz in the gin? Why, lady, my system's so full of preservatives that sometimes I get drunk off my own blood days after a binge."

"Are you sure there's ever been a period of days between binges?" Laura said. "You seem a little tipsy right now. I don't appreciate men barging into my hotel room and throwing around accusations and fluids."

"And I don't appreciate poison bein' put into the gin I steal."

"Again, I beg your pardon? You must believe me, Mr. Raving, I have no earthly idea what you're talking about. Would you mind taking a breath and starting from the beginning? I think we may be operating under some manner of miscommunication."

"Yeah, and the miscommunication is that I don't like bein' poisoned."

"You keep talking about poison."

"Yeah, poison."

"Let's start there. What poison, exactly?"

"The poison you slipped into that gin bottle I took the last time I was here."

"You stole a bottle of gin?"

I hesitated. "Okay, you got me there. But still, that don't rate poison."

"Mr. Raving, I really thought you were a better detective than this. How would I know you were going to steal a bottle of alcohol?"

"Nice try, sister, but my love of booze is legendary. It would be a pretty safe bet."

"Okay, I'll buy that. But how would I know which bottle you'd take? I have a larger selection of liquor here than most bars can offer."

"I...you...don't try to confuse me!"

"I swear to you, Mr. Raving—Stark—I had nothing to do with you being poisoned. And if it did have anything to do with a bottle of my gin, then it was put there by someone else."

"Yeah? Any ideas as to who else might want to poison me?"

Laura assumed a thoughtful expression for a moment and then her face stiffened.

"It might not have been meant for you."

"You been entertaining other disliked detectives in here?" I said, a pang of confusing jealousy coursing through my veins.

"No, Stark. I'm talking about me."

"Wait…you been talkin' to Ariel?"

"Who?"

"Hot tomato who works the bar on Third and Penryn."

"No, I—"

"And who'd want to poison you?"

"More people than you might think. Do you remember what brand of gin you stole?"

I thought. Normally, I wouldn't have remembered, but this had been top of the line stuff. When I told her, she nodded.

"Yes," she said. "That makes it clearer."

"As mud. Care to share?"

"That's my favorite brand of gin. In fact, it's the only kind I will drink, if I have any say about it. Unfortunately, most bars don't carry it because it's hard to sell, being so expensive. So I keep a private stock. Not many people know about this little eccentricity of mine. But I know of one who does."

"And that is?"

"My husband."

"Your—" Another stab of jealousy.

"—husband, yes. Ex-husband, really, although we never officially got divorced. He wanted it that way, as wives can't be forced to testify against their husbands."

"Why would he want to kill you?"

"For much the same reason he didn't want a divorce. He has things to hide. He's been threatening me for years to make sure I don't go to the police on my own, which of course I wouldn't, but he can be a paranoid man. Then, against my efforts, he found out that Gwen was being social with a private detective—you. And then we both had to go. We knew too much and, from his perspective, were turning against him."

"You don't sound surprised."

"I'm not. I know the man. I hate myself for not acting before tragedy struck. Part of me just couldn't believe he would kill his own daughter. Me, certainly. But not Gwen. Not Gwenny."

"He must have plenty of shit to hide."

"Oh, yes. Shit, bodies, hot cars, counterfeit money...back during Prohibition, it was illegal alcohol, often shipped in from Canada."

"A renaissance man."

"He has his sticky fingers in many forbidden pies."

"And where do you come in?"

"I was one of those pies."

I stifled a giggle.

She moved toward me and held out her hands. "Please, Stark, don't think ill of me. I'm not a criminal. My heart wasn't in it. I did for him, for Larry, my husband."

My pivots were tired, so I moved from the bar and took a chance on one of Gild's goofy chairs. It had mercy on me.

"You're gonna have to explain this a bit more, sweetheart. I'm not following."

Gild moved to sit in the chair next to mine. She

leaned forward, her hands gripping the arms of my chair.

"A few years ago, I was a lawyer. A good one. I was at the top of my class and I thought I was going to show the world what a top rate female lawyer could do. As you know, there aren't that many woman attorneys these days and there were even fewer then. But I stuck to my guns and put up with all of the hooting and catcalling. I kept my focus and got on at a respected law firm. A lot of the partners had their doubts, but the partner with controlling interest had faith in me and was committed to equality. Finally, he convinced the others to give me a shot at an important, high profile case. The police had finally captured the notorious criminal known as Uncle Larry."

My ears got pointy. I'd heard of this guy. A real cool customer, a dangerous joe, the cat's litterbox, the no-goodest of the no-goodnicks, the bane of justice everywhere, one of the most feared underworld movers and shakers to ever move and shake the feared underworld, a most stabby man, a—

"Anyway," Laura said, "to make a long story short, I failed at the job. The evidence against Larry was just too great. No matter what I did, the prosecution had an answer for it. They pulled out late evidence and the judge allowed it. Apart from being a strong case, it was a rigged trial. They were determined to put Larry away for good this time."

"They musta failed in the end," I said. "The last I heard, this Uncle Larry—your husband—was seen catching a plane to Mexico."

"Yes. They failed."

"So you musta figured out some way to change the verdict."

"I did. But I'm not proud of how I did it."

"You can tell me," I said. "I'm used to not bein' proud of stuff I've done."

"I tampered with the evidence. I did whatever I could. I stole important papers and paid off a witness to change his story. Even so, it was close, but the jury found Larry not guilty and the state had to let him go."

"You might as well tell me the end of story, sweetheart," I said. "I can tell there's more."

"My activities were found out, as they always are. I was disgraced and Larry was back on the wanted list."

"But why? Look, I ain't judging you, but there must be a reason why you would fiddle with the evidence."

"There were two reasons, really. First, I wanted to win the case for all of the women in law who were being overlooked and thought of as too dumb to make good lawyers. I wanted to prove that women weren't just secretaries and that we could roll with the best of the men. But I got the wrong case…and the wrong client."

"The wrong client?"

"That brings me to the second reason. Larry and I fell in love. I was mad about him. Even as the evidence stacked higher and higher, I just knew he was innocent. He had an answer for everything. He's a smooth talker, very intelligent and clever. A lot of charisma. That's how he's been able to stay at the top for so long in such a dangerous profession.

"Anyway, I wanted to believe him and I acted like a stupid fool. So I did what I did and got him off. But after it was all discovered, we were both in danger, so we fled the country, where Larry set about rebuilding his connections in preparation for a return to the States. I wasn't comfortable with it, but he knew just how to play me. He'd say, 'It's just for a while, doll. I gotta pay off my debts and make things square. Then we'll quit the racket for good and go straight, just like you say. We'll go to Europe and live like royalty.' Then he'd kiss me and hold me and I'd believe him, because I wanted to so much."

Laura was crying. Her face was streaked with that black stuff from her eyelashes. I leaned forward and put my paste-poles around her neck.

"Listen, sweetheart," I said. I was trying to be soft and vulnerable, and it burned my insides. "It ain't your fault. You just got caught up in life, ya know? I been there. I know what you're feelin'. I once had a dame that I'd do anything for. In fact, I *did* do anything for her. But in the end, I just let her down. My best just wasn't good enough. I know how it is. You think you know what's best, try to play the hero. Just comes back to bite you in the ass."

"Thank you, Stark. Thank you." Laura wiped her eyes. "I don't care what everyone says about you. You're a kind, sweet man."

"People are sayin' stuff about me? What're they sayin'? I'll paste 'em!"

She kissed me then, a good solid smack that left me stuck to the back of that slick chair like gum under a church pew.

"What was that for?" I said, a little breathless. The kiss had been good, but she had leaned forward and her elbow was digging into my groinal region.

"I guess I just felt like kissing you."

"No, I mean the elbow jab to my vitals."

"Oh! I'm sorry, Stark. That was an accident." She passed her hand over the area to soothe the pain.

"That ain't helping," I said.

She smiled and, goddamn it, if she weren't gorgeous with those eyes still bright from the tears. "Perhaps some time I can make my apology more...sincere."

"I've got time," I said.

"No, Stark, you don't. If Larry tried to poison me, then that must mean he had something to do with Gwen's death. And if that's the case, then he most likely is behind the disappearance of your friend. And if Larry has your friend, then...."

"Then we don't have much time."

"My husband is a cruel and twisted man, Stark. Even more when it becomes a matter as personal as this."

"I believe it," I said. "Any fella who would bump off his own daughter isn't to be taken lightly. Even so, I can't wait to paste him but good. You have any idea where he might have my friend?"

Laura thought for a moment.

"There is one place," she said. "It's outside of town,

deserted, remote. An old abandoned factory or warehouse. I've never been out there, but I've heard Larry talk about it. Apparently, it's the place where people go when they aren't coming back, if you follow my meaning."

"Of course I do," I said. "But just to be sure…what's your meaning?"

"Where they go to *die*, Stark."

"Seems unlikely. Most cats I know prefer to die in their own beds."

"Where they go to die *of murder*."

"Oh, right. Yeah. That's what I thought. Tell me how to get out there and I'll go have a look-see."

I left the Garish and stood on the corner of Third and Penryn. Too late, I remembered the condition of the mook's cab and how I'd promised to send a tow truck. I turned to go back inside and scout out a phone but saw the bastard himself, driving down the road in his old cab. The Plymouth wheezed and gasped, sounding like Jack Benny's Maxwell, but it was moving. Slowly, but still moving.

He pulled over the curb, just missing the fireplug, and grinned out the shattered window at me.

"I was just about to call you a tow," I said.

"Don't need one, pal! Need a ride?"

"Actually, I do. How'd you get this tub running?"

"Funny story," the mook said. "I was sittin' there waitin' for the tow truck and eatin' my sandwich, when I noticed the meat on the sandwich was all tough and rubbery. Musta been the end of the salami roll or somethin'. Anyway, I got this big idea, ya know, like one of them brain storms those smart guys talk about. So I gets outta the cab and raises the hood. There's steam goin' all over the place, but I look down in the engine and there ain't nothing wrong with it, exceptin' a coupla holes in the radiator and a snapped off hose. So I grab the bad meat from my sandwich and plug up the holes and wrap a slice around the bad hose, using mayo as the glue. Worked like a charm. Once I turned on the engine, the heat kinda made everythin' melt together. You wouldn't know any difference, if it weren't for the smell."

"You think it'll make it all the way out to Third and Penryn?"

"Third and Penryn?" The cabbie considered. "That's a distance. Yeah, I think so. Might hafta stop for another pack of salami along the way, though."

I piled inside.

"We're looking for an abandoned warehouse," I said. "I have reason to believe Tolstoy is being held there by an underworld crime boss."

"Leave it to me," the mook said. "I'll find it. I'm gettin' real good at findin' Third and Penryn." He paused. "This may be an awkward time, but ya think you could pay down your bill? I gotta get gas in this yacht some time, ya know."

I made a show of searching my pockets for money. As I ran my hands over my suit, I felt something, a bulge I didn't recognize. And it wasn't the one Laura had given me. This was something else. I reached inside and pulled out the packet of Gwen's letters. I had forgotten all about them.

"That a pack of money?" the mook asked. His eyes

widened with hope.

"Nah, letters," I said.

The light in the cabbie's eyes died. It was kind of sad to see.

"Come on," I said. "Let's drive. I'll get square with you once we find Tolstoy."

While he drove, I took the rubber band from around the letters and began skimming through them. I expected to see a lot of disgusting, personal bullshit, but that couldn't have been further from the truth. From these letters, it didn't appear that Gwen and Tolstoy had any sort of romantic relationship at all. Instead, it seemed more like a professional relationship.

Dear Mother,

I have spoken with Mr. Raving and he assures me that he can help us with this matter. He is familiar with Father's business and believes he knows a way to infiltrate the operation. Having done so, he plans to gather enough evidence to put Father away for good and break up the operation. Won't it be wonderful, Mother? We could be free, you and I!

Love, Gwen

Dear Mother,

Mr. Raving believes he is being followed, but he doesn't know by whom. He says he will begin the major part of his operation soon, before he is discovered.

Love, Gwen

Dear Mother,

I am sure that both Mr. Raving and I are being followed. Last night, I found my door unlocked, even though I am sure I locked it before going to bed. I also found deep shoe impressions in the fluffy carpet by my bed, as if someone had stood there watching as I slept. Also, my pretzels are missing.

Love, Gwen

Dear Mother,

The plan is going all to hell. I just found out that Mr. Raving isn't Mr. Raving at all! He's just a goddamn writer! What are THOSE good for! And what is worse, Father knows all about it. The writer is a friend of Mr. Raving and I just know we're all going to die. I'm going to the writer's apartment and try to talk him into leaving town before Father can have him killed or worse! Father must be furious and you know how stabby he gets when he's angry.

Love, Gwen

I was opening another letter when something slammed into the side of the Plymouth.

"It's those two stooges again!" the mook said. "Oh, this time, I'm really gonna paste 'em!"

"I dunno," I said. "They may be about to paste us. They've got tommies!"

Sure enough, the weasel was leaning out of his window and pointing a tommy gun right at us.

"Pull over!" he screeched. "Or I'll let ya have it so hard, you'll stop bein', ya know, alive!"

"What we gonna do?" the mook said.

"I'm not sure," I said. "It's kinda hard to take a threat like that seriously."

The weasel let loose a long burst from the tommy and I'll be damned if it didn't take half the roof off.

"Now *that* I can take seriously," I said.

The mook pulled over, barely missing a fireplug. We got out of the car but kept our hands up. The muzzles of the tommies never left us.

The mook looked at the hood, which was peeled back like the top of a sardine can. "I don't think I can fix this with salami. Now I'm definitely gonna hafta get a new car." He turned to me. "You really gotta pay your bill, pal."

"Yeah, sure," I said. "I'll pay." I suspected I wouldn't have the chance to pay him, since my future was looking grim. And part of me felt happy, because I really hate paying bills.

The big lug walked over and gave the mook a good clunk behind the ear with the butt of his submachine gun. The weasel chortled as the cabbie groaned and slumped to the ground.

"Okay, gumshoe," said the lug. "Your turn."

He gave me a smart lick on the head.

"Yeah, he tastes like a goner," the lug grunted. The weasel let off a giggle that sounded like a rabbit being stuffed with salami. Then the lug clocked me with his tommy and I saw stars and the next thing I knew, they were bundling me into the trunk of the sedan.

"Get in dere," said the lug. "We gots to get ya to da boss."

"Yeah, what Stan said," said the other, still wincing from that good pasting I'd given him. "Get in dere."

I tried to struggle but wasn't in the best of shape. What with the poison, the lugs, and the sidewalk, I was outnumbered. Not to mention my traitorous ankle. I resolved to have a word with it once this was all straightened out. My weakened condition and the determination of my two troglodyte captors overcame my desire to remain uncaptured. The trunk lid slammed down and I was in darkness.

I imagine one of the selling points of this automobile had been the storage space of the trunk. "Aaaand look!" the salesman probably said, grinning like a mongoose. "A spacious area to store the luggage for an entire family. Don't take a chance on the railroad to get your belongings safely to their destination. Take matters into your OWN hands!" But the guy had been fucking lying. It was cramped as hell. No legroom whatsoever. Admittedly, I'm the manly type, broad shoulders and long, toned sticks, but even so, I would've expected more from luxury. It was almost like I was sharing the space with someone.

What's more, it stunk worse than Caligula's anus. There was a sizable tear in the steel floor thanks to the encounter with the Plymouth, but it sure as hell wasn't letting in enough air or light to do me much good. It afforded me a nice look at the road below, so at least there was that.

I rolled over and felt around, hoping to find something breakable to make myself feel better and ease the tension. Breaking shit and pasting pusses were my top ways of letting off steam. And, brother, right now I had plenty. My hands grabbed something rough and pliable. Canvas. I reached into my pocket and pulled out my cigar lighter. A flick of the wheel and the rest of the trunk space lit up.

It was canvas alright, a long, rolled up piece of canvas with a length of rope wrapped around it several times and tied in the worst knot I'd ever seen. Someone had flunked out of the Boy Scouts. I unwrapped a corner of the canvas and held the lighter closer. A face stared back at me through the flickering light of the flame.

I closed the lighter with a snap, but the face stayed with me, burned into what my fictional predecessor called "the little grey cells." Right about now, I would've volunteered all of mine to science if I could forget what I'd just seen.

It was the dame from the alley. Here. In the trunk. With me. But she wasn't so gorgeous anymore. That angel face had turned an evil, sickly hue, like rice pudding left out in the hot sun. The red smeared lipstick was now just a sinful slash across spoiled innocence, perverse in its boldness.

Then it hit me. This morbid tableau was the dream that kept Ariel up at night come to a staggering, shuffling kind of life. That me being what I am and doing what I do would wind our daughter up like Gwen here. Yeah, of course I fought it, but I knew she was probably right. Even a loyal dog is still a dog, and not every dog is good around kids, even if that dog killed another dog to keep a gal safe, and that dog would give anything to be a good part of his daughter's life; you know what I'm saying? I don't know. I guess being locked in a trunk with a corpse gets me to rolling around the what-ifs and the coulda-beens. Suppose it makes me contemplative. I added that to the long list of things I'd be happier not knowing about myself. I'd drown it in bourbon later.

Gwen's eyes, the worst part, continued their stare, asking questions and demanding answers. They bored straight through me and asked why—why—why. Just as I had in the alley, I had more questions of my own than I had answers for her. And then I wanted out of that rolling cemetery in the worst possible way, even if I had to kick apart this fancy boiler bolt by bolt.

I could hear the lackeys up front, their voices resonant and muffled. They had been arguing about who had the keys, had switched seats a few times with much cursing and slamming of doors, but had evidently figured it out. Finally, the engine fired up and we were moving.

I took a breath. I had to admit I was spooked. But I also knew that losing my head wasn't doing me or Tolstoy any good. I had to calm the fuck down and think. I could see pavement whizzing by through the hole, the whistle of wind through its jagged maw the terrifying sound of time running out.

I thought fast and wriggled out of my pants.

Calmly, like an accountant in a laundromat, I began taking note of every turn, creating a mental map. Every time we rounded a corner, I shoved a bit of my rags through the hole. I didn't know exactly how fast we were going, but it felt fast. One right turn, a leg of my trousers. Hard left, an arm of my flogger. The wheels thudded over something bumpy—railroad tracks—and out went my undershirt. I prayed to Sam Spade someone would spot the trail and find my corpse. I didn't expect to get out of this alive, of course, but I'd be damned if I wasn't going get one helluva funeral, weeping dames in black, those little sandwiches with toothpicks in them, and a whole afternoon of twenty-one-rod salutes. The works. My slug-riddled ass was going be *present* for that shit.

We began to slow and I dropped out my last sock. I heard the crunch of gravel. The car stopped and I heard the slamming of doors. The lugs had a brief conference to figure out the trunk's lock mechanism.

"I think ya turns it to the right, ya know, like a doorknob."

"Ya don't turn doorknobs to the right, ya turn 'em to the left."

"And that's why you're always getting' stuck inside places, ya dumb gink. Ain't no doorknob in the world what turns to the left."

"Yeah? Well, maybe I'll just turn *your* knob to the left and we'll see how you like it?"

"You and what army?"

"Me and myself, dat's who!"

"You can't take me. You think you can take me?"

"Yeah."

"Yeah?"

"Yeah."

"Yeah?"

"Yeah!"

I kicked the trunk with my non-pivot foot. Facing these two stupid fucks was better than listening to them debate. I'd rather listen to a lecture by Hitler's sphincter than hear any more of their thick banter.

"Just open the trunk, ya goddamn cocksuckers!" I yelled.

I heard more fumbling and then the blessed light of day—not to mention fresh air—filled the trunk.

"Stop yer yellin'," Stan said. "Don'tcha think he should stop yellin', Merv?"

"I've a mind to shut 'im up for good," Merv said.

"Ooo, better not," Stan said. "The boss wouldn't like that. Although I wouldn't mind seein' this lout get what's comin' to 'im." He rubbed his jaw and glowered at me. "Pay 'im back for dat lucky punch he laid on me back in town."

"That was no lucky punch," I said. "I clocked you fair and square. And did you guys know you have a dead body in the trunk?"

"Is she still in dere?" Stan looked at his partner. "I thought I told ya to take care of dat!"

Merv averted his gaze and kicked at the dirt with his wingtips. "I mighta forgot a little."

"You forgot?"

"Yeah…just a little."

"How do you forget just a little? Either ya do or ya don't."

"Dat's the problem with you," Merv said. "Ain't got no sense o' nuance."

"Where the fuck you learn about nuance? You ain't been readin' a book, has ya?" Stan moved forward threateningly.

"No, honest! I ain't been readin'. I heard the boss say somethin' about it."

"Well, okay. If it was the boss, den I guess it's okay." Stan relaxed and patted Merv on the shoulder.

"Excuse me," I said. "I'm still here. So…the body?"

"Oh, right!" Stan used his patting hand to cuff Merv across the cheek. "I thought I told ya to take care of dat!"

"I was on my way to dump the body, just like the boss said, but I got kinda hungry."

"So?"

"So I was drivin' along and I see dis roadside stand selling tamales, ten for a nickel. You know I can't pass up a good deal, Stan."

"Okay, okay. Ya stopped for tamales. What's dat gotta do wit' the dead dame in the trunk?"

"So I eats the tamales, see, and a few miles down the road, I finds out why dey was so cheap."

"And just *why* was dey so cheap?"

"Dey was bad tamales, dat's why dey was so cheap. By the time I finished pukin' 'em up, I forgot all 'bout the dame in the trunk and just drove straight back here."

"Good Christ, Merv, you really are dumb, ain't ya?"

Merv hung his head. "Dat's what Ma always used to say."

"Spare me your sad childhood tales," I said. "How the fuck did you lamebrains get Gwen's body from the cops?"

"The boss gots connections," Stan said. "Somethin' about havin' a groundhog on da force."

"You mean a mole?"

"Yeah, dat's it! A mole! The boss gots a mole on the force."

Those two-bit crime flunkies down at the station, giving me shit about what I'd done, and all the while one of them was playing fast and loose with the law on behalf of the most notorious crime lord in the country. Was it O'Riley? McCarthy? I'd find out and, brother, I'd paste them but good.

"Listen, you two," I said, "I'd really prefer you just got on with whatever horrible things you're plannin' to do to me. If you're gonna kill me, then go ahead and do it so I can get on with my day."

Stan burst in clumsy guffaws. "Ya hear dat, Merv? He tinks we're gonna kill 'im!"

"Yeah, dat's rich," Merv, joining in the laughter. Then

he suddenly stopped and looked around in confusion. "Wait…we ain't gonna kill 'im?"

"Course we're gonna kill 'im."

"We gonna make 'im talk first?"

"Dat's right, Merv. We're gonna make 'im talk. It's what da boss wants, so dat's what we're gonna do."

My IQ had dropped a good twenty points just by listening to these two mugs. I didn't have that many points to spare, so I did my best to drown them out and instead took in my surroundings. We had driven in on a gravel road and a little distance away stood an abandoned warehouse, all smoked brick and boarded up windows. Wild vegetation grew around the building and, somewhere above, a crow loosed a halting, rusty cry.

I needed two things: a little more time and a .38. And a drink. So three things. An extra clip for the .38 would be a good idea, I figured, in case things got dicey. Maybe four things. A change of clothes couldn't hurt either. Five things. And shit, as long as I was wishing, I guess I'd take that cottage on the riverbank about now. Okay, six. The seventh thing I needed was a plan.

"So, hey, fellas," I said as jovially as possible. "Is Larry gonna come out here and join me in the trunk for our little palaver, or you gonna take me in to see him? Because if it's the latter, you two don't need to walk me in. I can go on ahead myself."

"Nice try, gumshoe," growled Stan. He and Merv each grabbed one of my arms and hauled me out of the trunk. With a goon on each arm, we marched up the gravel path to the warehouse's big steel double doors like the surliest wedding procession you ever saw.

"I promise I can make it worth your while," I said. I tried to give Stan a friendly nudge in the ribs, but he still had hold of my arm.

"Shut yer trap," he said.

"Oh, come on, can't we hear him out? Been a long time since my while was worth anything, Stan," said Merv, a forlorn and pleading look plodding across his big moony face like a tortoise with a mouthful of potato salad.

"Jesus Christ, okay. We'll lissen to just one—TWO, tops!—of this 'ere dead man's propositions 'afore we haul him through them doors to face the boss."

"Dese doors right here, eh, Stan?" Merv said, patting a door, his big moony face lighting up like some kind of spherical celestial body with a high albedo. "Dese doors what lead to the place where stoolies go in, but dey don't come out?"

"Yes, goddammit, dese doors right here, what leads into—hey, what in the name of Clem Kadiddlehopper you tryin' to pull, Raving? The fuck happened to yer rags?"

They'd finally noticed I was down to my undershorts. The watery evening sun played across my aging but Adonis-like physique, glinting off my alderman and waltzing through my thickets of virile chest hair. A soft breeze fluttered my skivvies. The crow called again.

"He's naked as a jaybird what still has his briefy-shorts on!" hooted Merv. "Hey, Raving, why you naked as a jaybird what still has briefy-shorts, huh?"

"Because he's a prevert, that's why," Stan said, wrinkling his nose. "Probably got a thing for dead dames."

They both kept hold of my arms but edged away slightly.

"What was it Ma said about preverts, Stan?"

"She said it's bad luck to chill off a prevert, 'cause their ghost will come back and tickle yer jewels in yer sleep, Merv."

The goons edged further away.

"But we ain't gonna kill him, right? The boss'll be the one ta ice 'im."

At this point, I was glad to have the repartee interrupted. One of the heavy doors suddenly swung open, banging into the side of the building. The noise shocked the goons into silence and the booming voice of a man out of patience made sure they kept it.

"Fee-fi-fo-FUCK!" it shouted. "What is the goddamn hold up? I've been watching you toad sphincters frog around out here for the last twenty minutes! I swear, if I hadn't gotten that loan from your ma when I was just starting out, rest her soul, I'd have daylighted you boobs years ago. Get him inside!"

Uncle Larry turned his glare on me. "And where the hell are his fuckin' clothes?"

L arry was a tall drink of water, and every bit as cold. A fine Polish suit painted his lanky figure black, his pins picked out in pinstripes. He carried a cannon on each hip, and draped across his broad chest, a bandolier of cigars. Cubans. The expensive kind, the classy bastard. He followed behind as the two goons led me into the shadowy warehouse, the click of his wingtips echoing off stacks of huge wooden crates, their tops lost in the gloom above. I could feel his gimlet eyes boring into the back of my skull, and the heat of his disapproval wilted my chest hair.

"Welcome, welcome, Mr. Raving!" he said, his voice viscous and malignant, like Satan's hotcake batter. "You've shown a stunning reluctance to do what's best for you, it seems, so I'm afraid I've had no choice but to intervene."

We came to a clearing in the forest of crates, an area lit by a few bare bulbs dangling on wires from above. In the middle, there was a big oak table, and at one end, Tolstoy sat tied to a chair, his face a purple mask of bruises. On the table in front of him was an empty glass bottle, spattered with red, lying on its side in a crimson-tinted puddle. Gin and blood. *Expensive* gin and *Tolstoy's* blood.

"Larry, you son of a bitch!" I roared. "You truly are a monster!" My voice cracked, and my entire body shook with rage. "How could you waste good gin like that? I'll see you hang for this!" I struggled mightily to free my paste launchers from his henchgoons, but they dragged me to a chair and shoved me into it.

"Tie him up, then go keep an eye on the door," Larry said with a wave of his hand. "And use our itchiest rope. I've got a treat for our friend here, but I wouldn't want him to be too comfortable."

The goons did as they were bid and withdrew. Larry wasn't kidding. This rope was some serious gas-station grade shit, abrasive as your ex-wife and twice as loose. Well, it started out loose, but Larry elbowed a goon aside and tied the knots himself. Shouted some stuff about having to do things himself if he wanted them done right. I was busy studying Tolstoy. It looked like they'd given him quite a beating.

"Tolstoy, old pal, how ya holdin' up? What'd you tell 'em?"

"Shut your talk hole, Raving," snarled Larry. The rope binding my hands behind me bit into my wrists as he yanked it taut.

"Ain't talkin' ta you," I spat.

"Ain't no difference, Raving," he spat back.

"Ain't none of your business, *Larry*," I spat again.

"Ain't gonna be able to stop myself from conkin' ya," Larry spat spitefully.

"Ain't gonna happen, redhot," I spat venomously.

"Ugh, you guys, that is gross," muttered Tolstoy, his voice thick and soggy, like he had a mouth full of socks. "You are spitting all over the table."

"Shut up, Tolstoy!" spat Larry.

"Shut up, Tolstoy!" I spat.

"I hate both of you," Tolstoy wheezed.

"Hush. I have a proposition for you two," Larry said, tenting his long fingers below his chin, the spitting image of villainy. "There's a good chance I'm going to kill one or both of you, but honestly, I haven't decided yet." He moved to the empty chair at the other end of the table, the one facing Tolstoy. "I'm something of a ruthless bastard, you see." He shrugged like there was nothing to be done about it. My pasters were itching to prove him wrong.

"I'm well aware of that, you twisted dingus," I hissed. "Ain't just any garden-variety flim-flammer can blip off his own daughter. And for what? What could possibly be worth that?"

Larry leaned back in his chair, tilted his head back and released a chuckle that sounded like Cerberus farting through a length of dusty lead pipe.

"Why, money, of course! Dough! Clams! Mazuma! Money is really great, and the vapid little twat was in my way. Much like you, Mister Raving. I'd have been content to live and let live, but you just couldn't stay out of it like you were told."

"I *do* hate being told what to do," I admitted.

"Of course. But when I found out she was chumming around with a *writer*, well, I had to act, didn't I?"

"You're talking out the wrong end of your gut, Larry. You're not making any sense."

He giggled again. "Oh, my, you're the worst. Sure, the law could have slowed me down, but only a little. A writer, though…a writer could crucify me in the court of public opinion, and that could really get in the way of me making dough. Besides, I have the entire police force in my pocket anyway!"

"Oh? And who might be your contact down at headquarters?"

"Like I'd tell *you*." Larry looked as if he might be getting ready to spit again. I hoped not, because my mouth was too dry to match him.

"Come on, Larry. You're probably gonna kill me anyway. What's the harm?"

"This is true," Larry said. "And I would enjoy letting you know how clever I am, even though by doing so, I commit one of the most common mistakes in criminal lore." He considered. "Okay, fine. I run the entire place, but my main squeeze is a highly respected sergeant by the name of William Briberson."

It was my turn to laugh. I squeezed out a good sardonic one. "Hurr! You mean Bribey Bill? Don't nuzzle my funny bone, Larry. That dirty turncoat's been on the force since I was, and everyone already knows about him. We just let him get away with shit every now and then because he's so fuckin' pathetic."

"That so?"

"Yeah. It's why he's got a nickname and all. Bill's like a mascot. They put him in film reels about workplace hygiene and shit. He's quite literally the only crooked officer in the city. One guy. So…bully for you." I felt relieved that O'Riley and McCarthy were off the hook. Sure, those were assholes, but I needed a little stability in my life right about now.

"No matter. He got me my traitorous daughter's body, and that's all I needed."

"Heh. Yeah, ol' Bill did like to pinch him some corpses. That takes me back."

"You live a horrifying life, Stark," Tolstoy interjected.

"Oh, thank you for reminding me, Tolstoy!" Larry said, nodding at the writer, a grin like a cat burying a deuce in a bed of petunias scampering across his chiseled face. "I've decided. I'll pin Gwen's murder on the wordsmith sap here, and I'm going to kill you, but I have a proposition for him first." He turned to Tolstoy, all traces of gaiety evaporating from his map. "If you can beat me in a round of poker, I'll off your buddy the gumshoe with a slug to the dome. Quick and clean. If I win, I get to feed him to my sack of rats a piece at a time."

I forced out another sardonic laugh. "That don't sound like your kind of odds, Larry. I heard you were somethin' of a high roller. Losin' your nerve in your old age?"

"What are you talkin' about?"

"The way you're playin' it, you don't stand to lose anything. Why not cut the shit? Make it death by rat if I lose and my freedom if you lose."

"That sounds like a horrible idea."

"Afraid you'll lose?"

"Ha!" Larry spat. I let him have that one.

"Any poker player knows they got to have skin in the game to make it worthwhile. Just wait until this gets out to your poker pals."

Larry squirmed and looked around at his goons.

"You trust all of them to keep their mouths shut?" I said. "You'd have to kill all of us in this room."

"You're making a mistake if you think that hasn't already crossed my mind."

"You hate your own men that much?"

"Nah, I just like killing," Larry said. "Monster, remember?" He paced back and forth, his evil genius hands held behind his back, somehow still steepled. "You do make a good point, as much as it pains me to admit. Any good poker game must have an element of real risk to be exciting. And I consider myself a gentleman in one thing only: poker. So I will agree to your terms. If I win, you die by rat. If you win, I will give you a fifteen-minute head start. After that, I will have my men hunt you down and feed you to the rats. Agreed?"

"Agreed. Oh, and one more thing. Just to make it really interesting, why not play me? Instead of Tolstoy."

"I'm afraid I cannot do that, Raving. As I said, I am a gentleman in poker. I have heard of Tolstoy's skill at the game. Apparently, he pays his bills with his winnings, much of which come from you. It doesn't seem sporting to play such an amateur. That would be as much of a stain on my record as refusing high odds."

"But I *let* him win all those games!" The words sounded hollow. I sank back in the chair and tried not to imagine a thousand tiny rat teeth tearing the flesh from my bones.

"Alright, Tolstoy," Larry said. "You ready?"

Tolstoy looked at me and tried to wink, but his eyes were nearly swollen shut and it looked more like a nervous twitch. Or maybe it was a nervous twitch that looked like a wink. Either way, I was fucked.

Larry snapped his fingers and Merv handed over a tray of chips and an unopened deck of cards. He showed the deck to both Tolstoy and me.

"You see? On the up and up."

"Hold on, Larry," I said. "Who's gonna be the dealer?"

"I thought Merv could do the honors."

"You think that's a good idea?" I said. "He's kinda—"

"Stupid? I know."

"Hey, dat ain't nice!" Merv said.

"I was going to say biased," I said.

"I don't think we have an impartial party in the room," Larry said. "And I can hardly allow *you* to deal."

"Don't trust me?"

"I don't trust anyone. And besides, Merv is far too stupid to cheat effectively."

"Hey!" Merv said. "Dat ain't nice!"

Larry looked at Tolstoy. "What's your game, Tolstoy?"

"Poker."

"Stud?"

"I like to think so."

Larry sighed. "No. I mean is stud poker acceptable to you?"

"Ah, yes. Merely joking."

"Seven card?"

"If you say so, but I think we'll need more cards than that."

"No! Seven card stud poker."

"Ha! Got you again. Of course, seven, er, card."

Larry peered at Tolstoy. "I can't decide if you don't know what you're doing or if you're playing dumb to throw me off my game."

"I don't need tricks to beat you," Tolstoy said.

"As you wish. Shall we impose a limit?"

"On what?"

"The betting! Good Christ!" Larry punched the table. "Stop with this ridiculous act! I have to deal with idiots all day long as it is."

"Hey, dat ain't nice!"

"Shup up, Merv! Say that one more time and it's off to the rats with you."

"Sorry, boss."

"I don't need a limit," Tolstoy said. "You're not going to bully me, Larry."

"As you wish." Larry pushed the cards and chips across the table. "Merv, give us each $1,500 in chips."

Merv picked up the cards and spent a good ten minutes getting the cellophane wrapper open. As he waited for Merv's stupid, fat fingers to open the pack, Larry drummed his gross, evil ones on the table.

"Okay, you guys," Merv said, pushing chips to each player. "Dis is gonna be a fair game, see? I'm gonna send out some cards to ya and you can tells me whats ya wants ta do."

Larry and Tolstoy tossed out their antes. Tolstoy's chips skittered across the table and plopped into Larry's lap.

"Fucking lugnut," Larry muttered.

Merv fumbled out three cards each, two hidden and one face up. I craned my neck to see the cards. Tolstoy showed an ace of hearts. Larry had a two of clubs. I wondered what Tolstoy's other two cards were. He tended to lose his head when he had an ace.

"I'm in for ten," Larry said, pushing out some chips.

Tolstoy frowned. "So do I put more money in now or what?"

I groaned. I was absolutely going to get eaten by rats.

"Call, fold, or bet," Larry said. "Come on, you know the rules."

Tolstoy called.

Merv delivered the Fourth Street card. Another ace,

this one diamond, for Tolstoy, a five of clubs for Larry.

"Can I put more in?" Tolstoy asked.

Larry nodded and Tolstoy pushed in ten. Larry called.

The Fifth Street card gave Tolstoy a nine of spades and Larry a seven of hearts.

"Hey, that was fun," Tolstoy said. "I think I'll do that again."

"I'm out," Larry said.

Tolstoy collected his winnings, looking smug and confident. The cards had given him the win and I knew Tolstoy well enough to know he was feeling lucky. This was going to end badly.

An hour later, they were still playing. All fears aside, Tolstoy was having the game of his life. It was weird how the cards favored the little guy. He never played this well at his apartment at the Mer. The little shit was using typically horrible judgment, but he couldn't seem to lose. He rode a pair of suited sevens into what looked like a sure bust, but at the last minute, pulled out a flush that gave him a nice chip lead. It didn't seem to matter what cards he held or what Larry's hand looked like. It was fun to watch, but with each hand Tolstoy won, the more nervous I became for the next round. This kind of luck couldn't last, especially when backed by a complete lack of skill.

I could tell Larry was about to snap his cap. With every passing hand, he leaned closer in, glaring at his cards with a gaze so intense I thought they might burst into flame.

"I can't catch a fucking break," he growled. "Fucking cards. Merv! You fucking with the cards?"

"No, boss. Too stupid."

"Oh, right," Larry said. "Deal the next hand."

Tolstoy had a ten and five, Larry had a pair of threes.

"A hundred," Tolstoy said, because of course he would.

"This is shit," Larry said.

"You out?"

"Fuck no, I call."

A ten for Tolstoy and a nine for Larry.

"I'm in for another hundred," Tolstoy said.

"Call."

A five for Tolstoy and a six for Larry.

"This fucking game is rigged!" Larry said.

"Five hundred!"

I could tell Tolstoy smelled victory.

"Call," Larry said.

"Hey, boss," Merv said, "ya think ya might wanna take it easy? The little guy's got two pair already."

"Shut up, you stupid shit, and deal the cards."

"I'm just sayin'—"

"Well, don't!"

Merv sent out the next cards. A six for Tolstoy and a king for Larry.

Tolstoy's face was all smiles. I could tell he was about to do something stupid.

"Tolstoy," I said. "Be careful. This hand may not be

what you think it is."

"Relax, Stark. This game is mine. You've seen me, I can't lose!" He pushed all of his chips to the middle of the table. "I'm all in," he said.

Larry looked at him. Then back at his cards. Then back at Tolstoy. Then he slowly cupped his hands and moved his chips to join the others.

"I'll see you."

The room was quiet, dead quiet. I instantly regretted using the term "dead quiet" and decided to never do it again.

Merv delivered the final card, facedown. Tolstoy checked his, then Larry. I watched Larry, but the man's face never changed. He put his card back down on the table.

"Mind showing us your cards, Tolstoy?" Larry said.

Tolstoy shrugged and flipped over his hidden cards. A four and a jack. Larry just sat for a moment and stared.

"Well?" Tolstoy said, eager to claim victory. "Show us. Don't be a sore loser." He began gathering in the chips.

A horrible, oily smile spread across Larry's face. He looked like a shark sitting down to a meal of baby seal blubber.

"I don't think losing is, pardon me, in the cards."

He turned over his first blind card. A nine. Two pair, nines and threes. Tolstoy still won. Then Larry turned over his second blind. Another nine. A full house, nines and threes. I was going to the rats.

"What the fuck!" Tolstoy screeched. "Both your

hiddens were nines?"

"It would seem so."

"That was quite a risk," I said. "How did you know you'd get that last nine? Until then, Tolstoy had you beat."

"It was my turn."

"I don't think that's how poker works."

"It does here," Larry said. He turned to his henchmen. "Would you mind bringing in my sack of rats? I'd like to introduce them to Mr. Raving. I think they're going to enjoy getting to know one another."

I struggled against my bonds. If only I could get my pasters free, I would show these goons one or two things, maybe even more. I heard a bunch of high-pitched squeaking coming down the hall. The rats.

They say your life flashes before your eyes just before you die. I'd really been dreading that, because most of my life I didn't care to relive. But a few things did come to mind that made me almost sorry the end was near. I wasn't afraid of dying, but the idea of being eaten by rats was not my idea of a good time. I'd always expected to go out in a blaze of glory, pasting out chin music with hot lead ripping the air. I'd get hit after taking out a dozen or so toughs and then lie back with my head against the tits of a beautiful dame, who would sing me songs as I drifted peacefully into that great black night.

It was romantic idealistic shit like this that always got me into trouble. Ariel floated into my mind. She was the beautiful dame and those tits were hers. I saw myself in a cop's uniform, a rookie, answering a domestic abuse call. Her husband was a real tool and I overstepped a little by roughing him up on the way to the station. I overstepped a little more by having a relationship with Ariel after she separated from her husband. And then I overstepped even more by killing the ex-husband when he wouldn't stop harassing Ariel and threatening to beat her to death. She had been a wreck, unable to sleep, crying all day, scared to leave her house. She just sat inside, in the dark, and hoped he would leave her alone. But I knew he wouldn't. I started trailing the guy and caught the guy stealing a bottle of booze from a pharmacy. I confronted him in an alley and put a bullet through his heart. Everybody on the force knew about me and Ariel. And no one believed my story about the guy charging me with a knife and that I'd had to kill him in self-defense. But cops protected each other, for the good of the department, they said, and there wasn't much of an investigation. Even so, I was suspended and quietly let go. I started the private detective gig to make money and because that was what I knew, but Ariel didn't want to be married and have kids with a guy who carried a gun and moved in the underworld, even if it was on the side of law and order. "One day you'll get killed," she'd said. "And you'd leave a child without a father. What's worse, your family could end up a target." She'd been right, of course, and I was seeing that play out. I'd beaten the odds for a long time, but the dead girl in the trunk had brought it all back. Still, I couldn't help but regret all the things I'd missed out on in life. And that was why I didn't much care to have it all flash before my eyes.

The ratsong grew louder and then Stan appeared, hauling a giant sack behind him. The bag seemed to be alive; it moved and pulsed. Larry stood up from his chair.

"Ah! My rats!"

Stan set the bag in front of him and Larry walked over. He stood in front of the rat bag and clapped his hands twice in quick succession. The squeaking, squealing, and thrashing stopped instantly and all was quiet.

"You see?" Larry said. "They really are quite well trained. For rats. In fact, they follow my instructions better than my own henchmen." He glared at them and they all looked down at the floor.

"So, what, you're just gonna stuff me in a bag of rats?" I hoped this to be the case. Given a crack at the rats in a confined space, I could paste those suckers but good.

"Oh, no," Larry said. "It's much more imaginative than that. Stan! Merv! Bring out the boiler!"

The two goons disappeared into the shadows at the far end of the building and I heard the squeak and scrape of rusty metal against even rustier metal, and metal against concrete. Slowly, a giant shape emerged from the gloom, metallic and lined with massive rivets. Stan and Merv pushed it along on an impossibly tiny cart. It looked as if the cartwheels weren't even moving and the giant contraption left a trail of rust and broken concrete in its path.

"And here it is, Raving," Larry said. "Behold my latest torture device. I'm really quite proud of this one."

"You're going to have to explain."

"Gladly! This is a modified industrial boiler."

"Modified?"

"Slightly, yes." Larry waved his hand at Merv, who in turn pushed open a sliding panel on the front of the boiler. "Ta-da!"

What I saw made my blood stop cold. Cut into the boiler was an opening in the shape of a man. One about my size. Dangling from the cutout was a leather suit, rife with buckles and straps.

"In case you haven't made the connection yet, allow me to explain," Larry said. "This is my rat feeding machine, the Brass Lass." He smirked horribly. "The victim, otherwise known as dinner, is strapped into this one-sided leather suit and then secured to the human-shaped opening so that there are no openings around the sides. Then the rats are poured through the hatch at the top of the boiler. Finally, a fire is lit under the boiler and, as the heat rises, the rats become more and more desperate to escape. Driven mad by the heat, they will eat their way through the victim into the open air."

I heard Tolstoy puking in the background.

"You must be proud of yourself," I said.

"Not really," Tolstoy said. "I've puked way more than this before."

"Not you," I said.

"I try to be modest," Larry said. "I do admit to a

certain amount of satisfaction. I have taken the medieval method of rat torture to an entirely new level. I tested out this device on an old employee of mine and it worked beautifully, better than I could have dreamed. Stripped him completely to the bone within minutes."

"You fed one of your own employees to the rats?"

"He was late bringing lunch."

"Well, you can't have that."

"Exactly. See, you and I are not that different. Under other, less crimey circumstances, we might have been able to work together."

"I'd never work with you," I said. "First, I don't like you. Second, I hate rats. Third, I really hate rats. And...whatever number comes after third, I just don't like you."

"They say the way to get over fear is to face that which you are afraid of," Larry said. "Let's see if that works in your case. Merv! Stan! Strap the gumshoe to the boiler!"

The goons dragged me to the boiler and began strapping me into the leather suit.

"Oh, I cannot wait to see how this all plays out," Larry said, pacing around with a beatific smile on his stupid, stupid face. "Will the rats eat first through the abdomen and target the tasty vitals? Or will they elect to strip the meat from your legs and escape that way, slowly working their way up until they're chomping at your dangly bits? It really is quite convenient that you came to us practically stark naked." He stopped pacing as if struck by a lightning bolt. "Oh! I do think I've made a funny!" He looked at me. "Stark Naked!"

"You're a scream, Larry," I said.

The goons had me strapped in and I resigned myself to fate. My pasters weren't going to be able to help me now.

"I think you'll be the one screaming," Larry said. "But don't worry. I won't think less of you. They all do it. Most have already started, simply from the sheer horror of it all."

"Fuck you, Larry."

"I think I'll save that for Laura," Larry said.

"Laura?"

"Yes. My ex-wife. I've been missing the old girl. And feeding someone to the rats always makes me frisky. I believe I'll pay her a visit once you've been reduced to a pile of bones."

"You're a credit to villains everywhere, Larry."

"And I thank you." He bowed so low he bumped his head on the floor. "Ouch. Merv! Punch Stan for making me bump my head."

Merv complied, Stan yelped, and Larry smiled.

"Better," he said. "Now pour the rats into the boiler. Careful not to stir them up too much. I don't want them getting too feisty before the heat is turned up. Otherwise, they might turn on each other instead of feasting on our friend."

"Friend?" Merv looked confused.

"The detective, you idiot," Larry said. "Stan! Punch Merv for being an idiot."

Stan complied, Merv yelped, and Larry smiled.

"Christ, I love my job," he said.

The goons lifted the bag of rats up to the boiler's hatch and began gently pouring them inside. Their little bodies hit the interior with echoing, metallic thumps and with each one, my throat constricted a little more. God, I hated rats. One brushed against the back of my leg and I involuntarily tried to jerk away, but the leather harness held me fast. I couldn't move. Even my head was immobile. I could breathe, move my eyes, and speak—probably so Larry could hear me scream—but that was the extent of my freedom. Claustrophobia crept over me and I fought to keep from losing my cool.

I heard the boiler door bang shut and a grating sound as one of the goons secured the latch.

"All done, boss," Merv said.

"Excellent. Hoist the boiler over the furnace and stoke the coals." Larry was wriggling in anticipation. "Oh, this is going to be lovely. Blood and gore all *over* the place!"

I heard the whine of winches and the boiler lifted into the air with a lurch that loosened my teeth.

"You might want to think about this, Larry," I said. "I'm not the only one who's on to you."

"Don't lie to me, gumshoe. I know all about you. You work alone. You don't even meet with most of your clients in person. Just use that little whore down at the bar."

"You leave Ariel out of this."

"Oooh, so the great Stark Raving has a weak spot, does he?" Larry smirked. "It's of no concern. You're married to the rats now, and they expect monogamy."

Machinery continued to whine and groan and the boiler moved with agonizing slowness across the enormous room until it hovered over a furnace pit. I looked down and could just make out the glowing coals. I could feel the heat. I wasn't sure what would be worse: getting eaten by rats or roasted alive once the heat was turned up. Rats. The rats were definitely worse.

"Get those coals going!" Larry barked.

I struggled against the restraints, but they were tight and seemed to tighten further the more I struggled. I forced myself to remain still and drew in a deep breath. The heat rose from the coals and warmed the air.

A rush of heat and a *whoosh* told me the coals had burst into active flame. It was only a matter of time. My feet felt like they were melting and the rats were getting restless. Their claws scrabbled along the metal interior and they began squeaking as the heat increased. Sweat masked my body and I could swear my feet were beginning to smolder. I felt a set of tiny teeth sink into the flesh on my lower back. I tried to draw away, but the leather straps held fast.

"It's just moments away now!" Larry said, hopping about and clapping his hands. "More fuel on the fire! More fuel!"

I heard a rush of flame and the rats increased their squeaking. Their desperation to escape the burning, smothering interior of the boiler turned them into a roiling, shrieking mass. Their claws scratched and tore at the metal. Another stab of pain shot through my back as a rat bit down. Then one on my neck. Claws ran down the back of my right leg and I felt the blood begin to trickle. Once the rats tasted the blood, it would go quickly. The horror and the heat began to take over and merciful darkness fell over my eyes. I could still feel the biting, the gnawing, the burning, the clawing...but it seemed to be happening to someone else, somewhere else.

I heard something. Something loud, like a gunshot. Maybe it was over. Maybe the rats had eaten straight through and the goons were shooting at them as they piled out of my gut. I didn't want to look, but I forced my eyes open and looked down, expecting to see my innards spilling out and rats climbing through my body. Instead, I saw Merv on the concrete floor, flat on his back with blood pooling beneath him. Another shot, and another and another. I raised my eyes and saw the old Plymouth flying across the warehouse floor, the mook at the wheel. There was ragged, Plymouth-shaped hole in the south wall. The mook had a bandage around his head and drove with one hand. The other held a pistol that spat lead as if it was going out of style. Ariel stood upright through the crumpled roof and blasted away with a shotgun, the casings flying out behind her and bouncing off the concrete. In the backseat, Laura Gild waited with a tommy gun and when the Plymouth screeched to a halt, she stood up and emptied an entire clip into dark interior of the warehouse.

"Stark!" It was Ariel.

I couldn't speak, but damn if I wasn't a little aroused. I'd been around the block a few times, and that was the most badass thing I'd ever seen.

The mook jumped from the Plymouth and ran toward the winch, but a few shots from the darkness sent him stumbling for cover. Ariel threw lead in the direction of the muzzle flashes and Laura jammed a fresh clip into her mill.

"We have to get him off of there! What the fuck is in that boiler?"

"Rats," I heard Laura mutter. "It's one of Larry's favorite pastimes."

"How do we stop it?"

"It might be too late," Laura said. "Once the rats go mad, it's difficult to stop them. If we could get to the winch, we could move the boiler away from the fire and set it down. Then we could unstrap Stark. But it looks like Larry and whatever remains of his crew are gathered by the winch."

"Bastards!" The mook emptied his pistol at the winch and dug in his pocket for fresh shells.

"We can't just let him die!" Ariel said. "He'd never let that happen to me unless he was being a real shithead." She ran for the Plymouth and jumped into the driver's seat. She stomped the gas and the car charged forward. It hit the shallow lip of the floor furnace and bucked upward, teetered, and moved slowly ahead, its back tires squealing on the concrete. Then it tilted forward and rolled into the flaming coals so that the rear of the car pointed up toward the boiler.

"Ariel!" I croaked. "Whatever the fuck you're doing, stop it!"

She clambered from behind the wheel and into the back seat, and then climbed the seat and crawled onto the trunk. She was only inches away when she reached up and began fumbling with the leather straps.

"That car's gonna blow!" the mook yelled. "Ya better move!"

I smelled burning rubber and knew the mook was right. If the Plymouth's fuel ignited, we were all done for.

"Ariel, just go. Save yourself. Get Larry and it'll have been worth it."

"Fuck you, Stark. You know you don't believe that. Stop trying to be a fucking hero."

She strained upward and managed to release my hand. I pulled it free and busied it undoing the rest of the straps.

"Be careful," I said. "Once I come loose from here, there's going to be a stampede of mad, bloodthirsty rats."

"Shut up and help me," Ariel said. "I'm not afraid of a couple of stupid rats."

It seemed like forever, but it must have taken less than a minute before my body peeled away from the leather harness. Ariel and I clung to each other and the side of the boiler as I twisted free from the straps. There was a rush of fur, fangs, and claws and a torrent of rats rushed from the opening and plunged downward into the furnace. A few managed to escape, but they were quickly put out of commission by the mook's big feet.

"Whoopee, now that was fun! Like a hoedown. But no foolin', Stark, that bus is gonna explode," the mook said. "It's done it before. You might wanna get a wiggle on."

"We need to get to that winch," Laura said. "We can use the attached pulley system to move the boiler away from the furnace and set it down."

Several bullets whizzed past their heads, reminding us all that Larry was still in control of the winch.

"It's over, Larry!" Laura said. "Give yourself up. Or just go. We won't stop you."

"Fuck you, Laura. You know how much I like my murders! The gumshoe dies. And then the rest of you can go to hell right after him."

I looked at Ariel. "There's no way we're getting off this thing before that car goes up. I'm surprised it hasn't already."

She nodded. "It's okay. Really."

"You didn't have to do this, doll."

"Yes. I did. And it's okay. I've always wanted to do something—anything—to repay what you did. And I'm sorry I—"

"We don't have time for that right now," I said. "There's only one chance to survive."

"And that is?"

I nodded into the boiler. "We have to go inside."

"Stark—if the explosion sends the boiler down into the furnace—"

"That's a distinct possibility. It's our only chance. I don't think you could jump from here and I know sure as fuck I can't, not in my condition."

"All right, Stark. If you say so."

We pressed close together and, as one, rolled into the boiler just as the Plymouth exploded in a ball of fire. The boiler shuddered and dropped, then caught and hung. I heard gunfire from below but couldn't see a thing. A slug whined off the side of boiler and I cringed to think what would happen if one of Larry's goons let loose a string of lead into the opening: we'd be cut to shreds by the ricochets.

The burning car had made matters worse. The boiler's interior was stiflingly hot. I could see why the rats would eat their way out. Fuck, I'd eat through a rat to get out of here. Ariel clung to me and I tried to think, but I was drawing a blank. I was just getting ready to make my peace when I heard the whirr of the winch and felt the boiler begin to move. The gunfire had increased. It sounded like Pearl Harbor down there. Laura yelled something, but I couldn't make it out. Then the boiler jerked again and started downward. I risked a glance out the opening and saw we were clear of the furnace. Someone was operating the winch. Then I heard a shot, one that stood out from the others, a single, deliberate round, and, as suddenly as it had started, the movement stopped and the boiler hung just a couple feet from the floor.

"I think we can drop down from here," I said. "Just

help me get through the opening."

Ariel grabbed my shoulders and pushed me halfway through. I crawled the rest of the way and let myself roll out and drop the short distance to the floor. Ariel followed close behind.

The gunfire had stopped. We heard the patter of footsteps, some cursing, and the crash of a door opening. A stab of sunlight showed Larry and a couple of henchmen disappearing through the door. A moment later, a car engine roared, tires spun gravel, and the engine noise faded into the distance.

"Fuck!" Laura threw the tommy gun onto the floor. "He got away."

I looked around. The mook, Laura, Ariel...

"Where's Tolstoy?" I said.

Laura pointed into the gloom toward the winch.

"Over there. He's the one who pulled you two away from the furnace. We tried to cover him, but Larry finally put a bullet in him."

I could see the little guy's body, dim and in grayscale, draped over the machinery, his hand still gripping the controls.

"I'll be damned," I said. "The little rat turned out to be a hero after all. How'd you guys find me?"

"We followed your duds," the mook said. "I didn't think a healthy man could sweat that much," he added in a soft mutter.

"It was hot in that trunk."

"That was pretty quick thinking," Ariel said, moving

closer and eyeing me like a hungry lioness. "And if it weren't for all those rat bites, you'd look pretty sexy right about now. If you were feelin' up to it, I might take you right now."

"I might just take you up on that, babe," I said. I double-checked to make sure the rats hadn't made off with my nightstick. No? Bully. "And never mind the rats. I just need a few drinks and I'll be good as new."

"I think a trip to the hospital might be in order before any sexual escapades take place," Laura said. Her tone seemed tense and if I didn't know better, I'd think she shot Ariel a dirty look or two. She sashayed over and placed a comforting hand uncomfortably near my southern region. "I'll take good care of you," she said. "You'll see."

It might seem crazy to complain about having two dames fight over who's going meet all your needs, but I had to admit I was feeling like shit. All I wanted was a few bottles of antiseptic and a few more bottles of booze. I'd lost a decent amount of blood, had almost been eaten by rats, almost roasted to death, and fallen from a dangling boiler. One might excuse my lack of romantic inclinations. Even so, I managed a tit grab on each of them before my eyes rolled back in my head and I hit the floor hard. I imagine it was worth it.

When I woke up, I lay in bed with the mook standing over me.

"How ya feelin', pal?"

"Where am I?"

"The hospital. We got ya all fixed up. The doc says you're gonna be fine. Just a few nibbles here and there. He said you could go home pretty much any time and that he didn't care and would I stop bothering him and that my breath was bad enough he was fixin' to offer me a room of my own."

"Uh huh. Swell. Where's everyone else? Where's Tolstoy?"

The mook shuffled nervously. "He bought the farm, pal. You remember. The warehouse?"

I did remember then. "And Ariel? Laura?"

"Them two dames?" The mook shook his head. "You got your hands full with them, pal. You'd think you was the only fella on earth, the way they been carryin' on. And me just standin' here!"

"Don't worry," I said. "They'll get over me once the excitement wears off. I've been down this road before."

"You poor bastard."

"It's a rough life. But, live and learn."

"That's what they say," the mook said, nodding sagely. "So what did ya learn this time?"

"Quite a few things," I said. "First, never let other people win at poker. Second, there's more than one situation where it pays to take your pants off. Third, never steal strange gin. Wait, no, scratch that. I'm leavin' that door open. And...third or fourth or whathaveyou, never take shortcuts through alleys on a stark and stormy night."

"We gonna go out on that joke?"

"You got a better one?"

"Nah," the mook said. "That'll do." He reached into his pocket and pulled out a flask. He held it out, his face questioning.

"You're a good friend, er, uh," I said, my mind scrabbling fruitlessly for a name I never learned. "Er, ya big mook!" I finished lamely. I topped it with a wink to show just how goddamn easygoing I was.

"Whoa!" the big guy said, his mouth agape in shock, his breath in pastrami. "You *are* a good detective. How'd you know my name?"

"Ha ha. What?"

"Yeah, it's Muhke! Harvey Muhke."

I snatched the flask from his hand. I raised it.

"A damn good friend, Harvey Muhke. And given tonight's events, looks like I'm down a friend. How do you feel about pulling replacement duty?"

"Yeah, all right," said the Muhke slowly and cautiously, "but only if you replace my Plymouth."

"Deal!"

I heard female voices from down the hall. It sounded like they were arguing and I thought I heard my name. I grabbed the flask, unscrewed the top, and took a nice...long...drink.

Made in the USA
Middletown, DE
26 July 2016